SKYBORNE SAPPER

World War II. Young Nick Burrows is embittered with himself, and society. Hoping to meet his brother Harry, he volunteers for the paratroops, but the brothers miss each other and Nick throws himself into the fighting in Tunisia with the First Army. When Nick is in action he's different — men trust him. His scheming keeps them alive in the events after the first parachute drop. When Nick finally meets Harry, he realises that he has 'found himself' at last.

DAVID BINGLEY

---◆---

SKYBORNE
SAPPER

Complete and Unabridged

LINFORD
Leicester

First published in Great Britain

First Linford Edition
published 2009

British Library CIP Data

Bingley, David, *1920 –*
    Skyborne sapper
    1. Brothers- -Fiction. 2. World War,
    1939 – 1945- -Tunisia- -Fiction. 3. Parachute
    troops- -Fiction. 4. Large type books.
    I. Title II. Chesham, Henry, *1920 –*
    823.9'14–dc22

    ISBN 978–1–84782–680–0

Published by
F. A. Thorpe (Publishing)
Anstey, Leicestershire

Set by Words & Graphics Ltd.
Anstey, Leicestershire
Printed and bound in Great Britain by
T. J. International Ltd., Padstow, Cornwall

This book is printed on acid-free paper

1

An overloaded, battered American Dakota with 'Yankees for the World Series' chalked on its undercarriage shuddered and rattled as its engines opened to full throttle in an effort to take off.

It carried a score of soldiers wearing the camouflaged green jumping smocks and helmets of the British Parachute Division, sometimes known as the Red Devils. The bomb racks held cylindrical containers of stores; loaded with Brens, food, ammunition and other essentials, they weighed three hundred pounds each.

There was no wonder that this plane, like the other two score with it, had difficulty in leaving the ground.

Since dawn the paratroops had worked incessantly, lugging their equipment across an airfield near Algiers, and making up for a crop of last minute hold-ups caused by ground transport difficulties and the late arrival of several transport planes.

It was late November, 1942. Earlier in the month, the Allied First Army, commanded by General Anderson, had come ashore along the coast of Algeria to help the British Eighth Army which was operating against the Afrika Korps, further to the east. With the First Army's arrival, hopes were mounting that the Allies could finish the seesaw desert campaign, and drive Marshal Rommel's forces out of Africa for good.

Forward elements of the First Army in Tunisia were already heavily engaged. To complicate matters, the build up of forward troops and the transporting of their equipment and stores were being considerably hampered by fighters and bombers of the Luftwaffe, and highly mobile groups of hostile armour.

In an effort to assist struggling units of the First Army, parachutists had been briefed to make a two-pronged attack. One strike was against a small and isolated airstrip used by the Germans when their true base was receiving attention from the Allies. The other target was a tank workshop and harbour further to the east, situated between Zaghouan and Hammamet. This strike was a much more formidable task, calculated to need the whole outfit which was several hundred strong, except for one small key section.

Finally, this plane, crewed by baseball fans, and carrying the key section, clawed its way up to a respectable altitude, bearing its cargo of twenty men. The passengers remained slumped down in their bucket seats either side of the fuselage, thinking of the brief gay times they had had on the lush fertile strip of coastal Algeria which was slipping away beneath them.

★   ★   ★

Weeks of preparation had gone into the training for the coming drop and the subsequent action, but no mother's son was immune from an inner queasiness brought on by excitement and tension.

Private Nick Burrows, a darkly handsome Sapper with a permanently bluish chin, was right aft on the starboard side.

3

His stomach was flapping and he felt that any unnecessary movement on his own part would make him have to call out for the bucket and lose the breakfast which he had kept down this far.

Nick was just twenty-two years of age. In action, he was usually the master of himself and thoroughly reliable, but at other times he was introspective and rather hard to get along with.

Prior to joining the army, he was a restless, wilful and impressionable young man who could not settle to anything for very long. He left Burrow shipyard and his engineering apprenticeship, ducking a reserved occupation in an effort to escape from a home where a new stepmother failed to understand him.

His father, whom he had loved dearly, had been torn between his unmarried son and his new wife. In May, 1941, Nick's father and stepmother were both killed when a bomb demolished their home in the shipyard town.

Nick was in the Middle East at the time, and unable to get compassionate leave for the burial. Later, however, by volunteering for the parachute brigade, he had managed to get back to England to train for his new job, and to try and see his older brother, Harry.

To his disappointment, he missed his brother. Harry, a schoolmaster, and a good friend and companion to Nick before he married, had volunteered for the new Reconnaissance Corps, and gone overseas.

Since his arrival in Algiers by battleship, Nick had entertained a secret hope that Harry would reach the same base with a Recce outfit intended for service with the First Army. Again he had been disappointed. Now, hunched up in the plane, he was comforting himself with the idea that Harry had joined the Eighth Army, and that their paths would cross when the two Allied armies converged.

⋆　⋆　⋆

The airborne strike force thundered on through the cloudless sky, heading steadily eastward. Down below, the fertile land gradually gave way to rolling foothills, the slopes of which were studded and whiskered with rocks and thorn scrub. It was devoid of human habitation. Sometimes the veteran American transports maintained formation with ease; at other times they coped rather hurriedly with air-pockets of differing densities.

At a higher altitude, Lightning fighters, glinting briefly in the brassy sun, kept guard over the heavier and more ponderous transports.

The foothills came to an end. Vegetation disappeared altogether. Suddenly the world beneath the plane was a mass of threatening rock in the shape of jagged ridges, interspersed with narrow defiles of peculiar depth and shape. The aircraft followed a natural corridor through the menacing pinnacles which were populated only by huge birds of prey. These feathered creatures left their eyries and opened their flesh-tearing beaks to shriek in anger at the disturbance, but the sound of aero engines blotted out their utterances.

Soon, that far flung eastern spur of the Saharan Atlas was negotiated, and the ground receded as the rocky fastnesses fell away astern. Foothills appeared again, and finally a patchwork of tiny Arab dwellings and cultivations sewn into an undulating stretch of earth like a brown blanket.

★   ★   ★

A good two hours after take-off, the American crew chief suddenly appeared in front of the forward partition. He mopped his hollow cheeks, took a look around and started to walk aft, taking great care not to foul the statichute cords already trailing from 'chute packs to the central rod close under the deckhead.

Here and there, he administered a gentle shake to men deep in sleep. To others he nodded and grinned, halting the rhythmic motion of his lantern jaw as his teeth worked on chewing gum. Soon he was back where he started, and leaning on the senior officer present, Captain Joe Burns, second in command of 'M' Company.

Their conversation came to an end.

Behind this pair, passengers were now moving restlessly. Three men in succession called for the bucket and vomited. Others rose to their feet, pulled a length of cord out of their packs and hooked themselves to the 'chute bar.

Burns stood up to give his preliminary instructions, which were really unnecessary. All the men wanted to know were details about the 'drop' if there were any they had not been told.

'Ten minutes to go, lads,' he called loudly, in a West Riding accent which had once been broader. 'The Yank fighters have left us now, but if we have any trouble when we start to float there's an outfit of Spitfires not far off. Anybody not hooked up, do it now. Check an' double check, because once you step out there's no comin' back!'

They had heard this last remark many times before, but they suffered it once again from the straightforward Yorkshireman, knowing that he suffered from pre-jump nerves just as much as anyone else. They reacted quickly to the order to 'Stand up' and allowed him to pass down the line, giving their jumping equipment an extra check. This again was unnecessary, but it served to take the sting out of pre-jump nerves by giving the men confidence in their apparatus.

At last, Burns was back at the front. The warning light glowed red beside the head of the crew chief. Burns crouched and was out of the jumping door, leaving his static line to crack against the rear edge of the frame. Number Two took his place and disappeared. The figures dwindled in front of Burrows. The fuselage was spawning its green caterpillar babies with a vengeance.

Nick gulped and shuffled forward again. He felt as though two hostile regiments of soldier ants were slowly and deliberately eating their way through his vitals from opposite sides. The man right ahead of him had a red spot on the back of his neck. It vanished as the fellow crouched, pushed off and spilled backwards in the slipstream.

Nick followed. His statichute line rapidly grew taut, and the first sections of his parachute were hauled out. Another

few somersaults and the canopy shuddered and started to open. The miracle of
arrested descent was happening all over
again, dispelling the immediate tension
which always builds up in a man around
the time of the jump.

Burrows opened his mouth and sucked
in air. He glanced below him and grinned
crookedly. The sky was full of parachutes
which had already blossomed. Mostly,
they were of the standard colour, but here
and there the pattern varied as coloured
'chutes usually attached to containers
drifted towards a ploughed field.

Scores of men had already landed.
Some were pulling in their collapsing
parachutes; others had already done this
and were stepping out of their harness.
Every time Nick blinked, a man hit the
ground with legs together and went into
the roll which distributed the shock and
protected his more vulnerable parts.

The floating parachutes beneath him
grew steadily fewer. Soon, he was in the
last twenty feet of descent with nothing to
fear except the hard ruts and ridges of the
ploughed field. One boot sank into a rut

and the other scraped a ridge. He made a rapid adjustment, and rolled onto his shoulder, continuing his motion until he managed to check the heaving silk with a foot in each of two adjacent ruts.

He came to his feet, breathing hard and wondering if he had any special sprains which would prevent his going ahead when the others moved. He tested his limbs gingerly and found himself to be quite fit. Slipping out of his parachute harness and jumping jacket, he clipped a magazine into his Sten and looked round for Ginger Potts, the man who had jumped before him.

For a minute or more, he could not see Ginger, and his stomach started to heave again.

'Over 'ere, sir!' a blunt north country voice called.

Nick was relieved. That was Potts calling to Lieutenant Casson, whose batman he was. The Lancastrian was kneeling on a ridge some seventy yards away, his hands on his hips and his deep set eyes glowering at a container, the end of which was resting on mud in the bottom of a shallow gully.

The subaltern, some twenty yards away on Nick's right, started to chuckle. He was sandy-haired, freckled and stocky. His legs were short and his chest deep. His happy-go-lucky attitude, however, was often deceptive. As he chuckled he was thinking that Potts had to have something to grumble about. Having the container land in this messy spot would probably put him on his mettle for the rest of the trip.

Casson hurried to join his batman, and Nick went after him. The latter arrived in time to help drag the container clear. Two privates hurried up with the trolley, which enabled them to shift the cylinder to a section rallying point. Out came the Brens, the extra ammunition, the first aid gear, the food and the action rations.

Meanwhile, Corporal Johnson, a Roman-nosed scouse from Liverpool, hurriedly mustered the men.

'The whole of the section's intact, sir, but I've heard that Captain Norris, the Sapper officer, who was supposed to go with us on our special jaunt has broken his ankle. Have you heard anything about it?'

Casson's sandy brows rose. 'Cap'n Norris with a broken ankle? But he was supposed to do the airfield demolition and make a big show of it, as though we were attacking in large numbers! Point is, what do we do now?'

'Company H.Q. seems to be over on the left of the farm, sir,' Potts advised calmly.

Casson nodded. The farm was a jumble of stone buildings with an outer perimeter of cactus. It raised livestock, crops and an extensive olive grove. No doubt the other paras would have plenty of time to make use of its amenities, but not the boys around him.

The subaltern cleared his throat. 'I'll nip over and report to the O.C., lads. You stay right here and see about a brew up. I've got a feeling they'll be wanting us on our way as soon as possible, regardless of casualties.'

He stared in rather puzzled fashion at Nick, who was the only other man with the 'stick' who had engineering training.

The rest were simply airborne infantry. Nick met his gaze without flinching, and presently Casson shrugged and hurried off. By this time the parachute field ambulance unit was busily coping with the usual crop of jumping strains and bruises. By hurrying, he overtook Captain Norris, who was stretcher-borne and heading for the gate of the farm.

Ahead of the stretcher was the flying M.O., and not far behind was the chaplain who acted as his assistant. Norris was in pain, clenching his teeth on his red beret. Talking in short, sharp sentences he made it clear that he regretted his accident and the extra responsibility it would throw upon Casson. He wished him well for the future. The chaplain stepped around the subaltern, gave him a friendly pat on the back, and suggested a visit to Company H.Q.

Casson located the wireless section by a hedge, and near it he encountered Major Alec Dunstable, a regular soldier who revelled in the chances the war gave for action and accelerated promotion. Dunstable was about average height and slimly built. He was noted for his stamina, having been a top-class hurdler in the thirties. He acknowledged Casson's salute, grinned, smoothed out his fair moustache and fell into step beside him.

From far to the north came the muted crash of shells. Both men hesitated for the length of one step.

'Casson,' the C.O. began, 'they say the occasion produces the man. You'll know about Captain Norris' injury? Well, I can't really spare another Sapper officer to take over his job. How would it be if I asked you to cope without him? You have another Sapper with you who could handle the demolition?'

Peter Casson hesitated, having personal doubts about Burrows. All he knew was that Potts, his batman, thought Burrows a queer cove. This was not much to explain to a C.O. Dunstable noted his hesitation and interpreted it as lack of personal confidence. He shot his subordinate a sharp glance. Casson reddened behind his freckles.

'I — I'm sure we'll cope somehow, sir. It's just that, well, I don't know much

15

about Burrows, the Sapper.'

The Major cleared his throat excessively. 'Well now, here's your chance, old man! Get to know him! After all, you'll be in his company for twenty-four hours before you do your strike. Remember what I said about the occasion producing the man. Draw the best out of him, eh?'

Casson forced himself to look confident. The Major's pep talk ran out. They shook hands and wished each other well before parting.

★   ★   ★

'Was I right about the Captain's accident, sir?' Corporal Johnson asked. His restless eyes explored the familiar face in an effort to elicit the information.

'Yes, the Captain's a casualty,' Casson admitted. 'Meantime, how about some char for your new C.O.?'

Potts came up chuckling with the tea. 'Didn't I say to you blokes my officer always drops on his feet?'

The men grinned and showed their approval while the subaltern sipped his tea and warned them to be ready in ten minutes. At the appointed time, the section gravitated towards the farm with their Everest packs slung over one shoulder, as though they were joining the rest of the outfit and digging in for the night.

As the French farmer and the last of the Arab labourers moved beyond the cactus fence, however, Casson led the way to a dry gully behind a low thorn hedge. One moment his men were there, and the next all of them dropped out of sight.

Fifteen minutes later, they left the gully and made their way through a field of high yellowing grass, aiming for higher ground. Casson led and Johnson brought up the rear. In between them were seventeen men, all heavily laden, and carrying in turns two Bren guns.

Presently, Casson became aware of a man dogging him closely. He glanced back, and Nick Burrows said: 'Sir?'

The subaltern reduced his pace and Burrows overtook him.

'Sir, I wanted to ask you what's going to happen about the actual demolition at the airfield now the Captain's dropped out.'

The officer yawned. 'That's what we're all wondering, Burrows. The way the C.O. sees it, the occasion produces the man. We'll have to depend on you, very largely.'

Nick Burrows' throat dried out. Rebellion was never very far from his lips. Now, he protested. 'But that's not fair, sir! I'm only the equivalent of a private! I shouldn't have to take the weight, really!'

Casson glared at him. 'As far as I'm concerned, Burrows, you represent the whole of the Corps of Royal Engineers on this jaunt! You're the only one among us with any engineering training! And in any case, we aren't asking you to build anything! It's all destructive work! I should have thought that suited your temperament!'

Nick sucked in breath for an angry retort. With a big effort, however, he managed to restrain himself and resume his position in line. He was thinking rather savagely that a lot could happen before they reached the airfield.

Somehow, the foot-slogging through the foothills calmed him. In spite of the heat and the heavy weight of his pack, the exercise reminded him of tramps with his older brother through the Lake District. Soon, he was actually in step with the short-legged officer in front. They were making good use of a goat track when the daylight began to fade.

As though anxious to do business before darkness, two Stukas whined out of the north, causing the isolated section to drop flat in their tracks. The planes went straight on by, and suddenly flares lit up the sky further south.

During the wait, Private Potts asked: 'What do you make of that, sir?'

Casson sniffed. 'I don't rightly know, Potts. Perhaps their radar is functioning late, or someone we flew over has telephoned in information. I reckon somebody was bound to come and look, don't you?'

Potts stopped scratching his chin and nodded. He was about to say something else when the sounds of two small bombs exploding carried to their ears. Casson

19

stopped a noisy wave of speculation with a gesture. He listened hard, but could not hear any sound which suggested retaliation from the ground. He heaved a sigh of relief when the Stukas came away from the area in which the dropping zone was located and faded away towards the north.

'I don't reckon they spotted us,' he opined. 'We'll go on for an hour or so until we get tired, or the going deteriorates. Then we'll dig ourselves in till dawn.'

As he struggled to his feet, he noticed that crooked grin back on Burrows' face and wondered if, after all, he was looking forward to the coming action.

2

The way things worked out for Lieutenant Casson's small party, they were glad to fall out after a further ninety minutes of walking with loaded packs. Sunset was still a while off, but the track along which they were progressing was in shadow because the sun, well over towards the west, was behind the formidable mountainous backbone of Tunisia.

Casson felt the need to assert himself when they stopped and put down their packs. 'I would have liked to go on further, men,' he explained, 'but darkness is not far off and our campfires will show over a good distance at this height. If they are seen, the local Wogs will guess at once what manner of men we are. No shepherds or goatherds come up here. Even the goats seem smart enough to keep away. I have a feeling it will get cold in the night. Just the same, I want the cooking fires dowsed as soon as the meals are prepared. Is that understood?'

His eyes scanned the rest of his outfit. He received their grudging approval of his scheme, while the paratroopers vied with one another to build the fires and share the cooking. This was not the sort of terrain where a man went off with his 'townie' and talked about peacetime.

When a useful group had taken over the preparation of the meal, Casson began to scratch his head. 'I want half a dozen volunteers to make a shallow ditch over here behind the camp site!' he explained, in a loud voice.

Ginger Potts thought that his bloke was going to make himself unpopular before they reached their objective, but he figured it could not be helped really, seeing as how Pete Casson was the only officer present. Doubtless all would be forgiven when they went into action and all the present tension went out of them. It wasn't so much knowing they were in the middle of enemy territory that made men jumpy and irritable. Rather it was knowing that the testing time lay a long way ahead.

The volunteers for the trench were slow in coming forward. The men probably thought it unnecessary on this remote hillside. Potts could see his officer tensing up at the delay. With a slight shrug of his shoulders, the batman stepped forward and showed himself willing for the new chore. Reluctantly, other men strolled forward behind him.

Casson began to grin. He could see seven men. If he pretended his arithmetic was not so good he could have seven men do the chore in less time. On the other hand, the seventh man could probably count up to seven, and if he was not turned away he would probably nurse a grievance.

The subaltern pointed to the seventh man. 'All right, Burrows, you just timed it nicely. You're number seven. You won't be needed.'

Most of the squad turned to glance warily at Burrows. The latter shrugged. 'I wasn't intending to volunteer for trench digging, sir. I wanted to ask if you weren't going to post one or two sentries.'

Officer and volunteers heard a slight

gasp go up from the others. Casson looked down the slope into the gully beneath them. He appeared to consider the matter very carefully. The shadows were deepening steadily. Casson removed his head gear. 'All right, Burrows, thanks for the suggestion. I think if anyone decided to creep up on us from below they could find out all there is to know about us in no time. Perhaps you'd keep lookout from the forward end of the site for a while? I'll take a short spell at the other end myself. I've got a few ideas to sort out.'

A paratrooper preparing the food pushed binoculars into Nick's hands, and in that situation he had no excuse to duck the tour of duty which he had suggested himself. Fastening his smock up to the neck, he walked forward until he found a sizeable boulder with a useful niche behind it. The main planes of rock were so placed that he could easily see along the bottom of the valley in the direction in which they had been heading.

He settled himself in, took a good look round in all directions, and decided that the binoculars were as good a pair as he had ever handled. Nothing stirred except a small animal or two, and a few wild birds. It suited him to be away from the rest with his thoughts, for a while, although the glow of the cooking fires had an attraction all their own as the temperature dropped.

He thought of himself scouting as a boy up the Lake District. Revelling in roughing it on a hillside above Windermere, or Coniston. In those days, life had seemed great, except that there was no chance to get the knees brown in an area which received more rainfall than most.

The calling of men to their mates made the fires seem more homely. Nick wondered how and why it was that he always saw himself as a loner, a man away from the rest of the herd. He supposed it had something to do with his stepmother, and the death of his father and stepmother while he was abroad. Around the time when compassionate leave to attend the funeral had been refused, Nick had talked with a fellow who was an orphan. They had been in Cairo at the time, and the two of them had knocked about together. The day came, however, when the orphan told Nick he would have to toughen up, accept the fact that his parents had gone and prepare for a future without them. With nobody waiting for him in civvy street when this lot was over.

The well-wisher had bluntly repeated his advice on two or three occasions, but Nick was not ready to accept the true facts and the repeated advice had led to bitterness between them. They had parted in anger and never sought one another's company again.

Nick had thought over the differences between them many times since Cairo. It didn't seem to make any difference to his attitude of mind. Harry had joined up, received a commission; father and step-mother were dead, and that was that. An orphan could talk, because he had grown used to not having folks from the earliest age. The lone sapper sighed.

He blinked his eyes, panned the glasses slowly round the valley, and licked his lips. He pulled a small tin out of his smock, and rolled himself a cigarette which tasted good even on an empty stomach. His thoughts slipped back to Barrow shipyard, and the engineering apprenticeship which he had ducked out on to join the Army.

Seventeen thousand men, and a few women worked in that shipyard. They moved in before seven-thirty in a morning and knocked off at twelve. At one in the afternoon, they resumed again until the buzzer went after five o'clock. Then, unless they were working overtime, they charged for the outer gates and did not ease down to a walk until they were well over the high level bridge and heading for the buses and trains.

Ever since the war had started the engineering sheds had been blacked out. The electricity was the only light the workers saw until they came out again. In winter, a man could go to work in the dark, and come out again in the dark at a little after teatime.

The shipyard and engineering workers moaned and grumbled as much as any man in the armed forces, but most of them still thought they were a jump ahead of the armed forces because they were in a reserved occupation. Some built locomotives, others gun mountings for ships. Yet another lot actually built submarines and aircraft carriers, and repaired damaged warships.

There was that occasion when a destroyer had come in from Narvik with one third of its length missing. Stern first, at two knots, all the way from Norway, and the first thing in dock was to open up the compartments right aft of the damage and remove the browned bodies of the personnel caught and roasted in there . . .

Nick shuddered. If he hadn't been so restless, he might still have been in the shipyard and home every night, instead of floundering about the trouble spots of the world and not knowing what the future had in store.

At a time like this, for instance, he might have been coming out of the Ritz Cinema instead of straining his eyes in fading light to try and catch sight of non-existent Arabs, who might make life far more unpleasant. It occurred to him that his watch-keeping was not all that efficient. With a shrug, he put aside his thoughts and used his eyes more thoroughly.

The next distraction was when a man chewing a hot sausage came along to relieve Nick so that he could get his food. He nodded, moved to the nearest fire and ate ravenously. Casson was firm about putting out the fires shortly after the men had finished eating. During the night, an event occurred which gave the grumblers grounds for thought, and boosted the subaltern's confidence.

Two German planes idled over the line of their day's tramp. About a mile to the south a flare was dropped which illuminated a large area as bright as day. Less than a half mile on the other side, a second flare dispelled the darkness. The two heavy droning planes flew over the area with their crews probably using night glasses in an effort to locate enemy formations.

By that time, however, the paratroopers were all turned in except for the guards, and not so much as a glowing ember remained of the fires to give away their position. Casson, himself, made one or two scathing remarks about Germans in general, and the *Luftwaffe* in particular, and his men listened and laughed and decided for themselves that young Cass was wise beyond his years.

Needless to say, the outfit remained undetected, and reveille was the next disturbing event. Breakfast was made and consumed, and the party moved off with their morale high. During the middle of the morning, they rested on the side of a spur, overlooking a small hamlet of adobe dwellings.

This was cautiously by-passed. During the afternoon, they needed to make another diversion, this time to slip around two adjacent farms. Arab children could be seen skipping about in the yard of the second one, and a buxom girl in her late teens had several pairs of glasses trained on her without her knowing. During most of the day's trek, the paratroopers had kept calm, but as the afternoon moved into early evening, the nerves of their stomachs began to knot up once more.

Nick Burrows, who was still trudging

along behind the subaltern, began to feel curious eyes on his back again. The sensation made him nervous and apprehensive. He no longer thought that it was unfair to expect him to have all the responsibility for the demolition at the airstrip. Now, he worried about whether he would be able to do a good job. He had received instruction, in training, of course. But to do a really first class job, he felt he would have to have his say about the actual assault.

Around five o'clock, the unit was halted on a spur of the foothills at a place which overlooked the airstrip. One after another the men dropped their packs and patiently waited for a chance to look through the binoculars.

The airstrip was small in total acreage. In shape it was like a rectangle with the corners rounded off. A narrow concrete perimeter track had been built round it, and two straight runways cut across it in parallel lines. The windsock was strategically placed, and most of the buildings were on the side towards the east.

First there was a one storey building which looked like a guardhouse. Then there was a gap before the gaping mouths of four hangers, all built in one block. Beyond the hangers was a grassed over space with mounded tops which could have housed air raid shelters, and finally, perhaps a furlong beyond the grassed mounds was a substantial single-storey block of offices, billets and stores. Extra blocks jutted out at the back of the main line and made the establishment look as if it might have been busy at one time.

Ginger Potts had dropped down beside Casson. 'How about that criss-cross fencing, sir? Will it 'ave electricity through it, do you think?'

Casson turned and eyed his batman. 'I don't think so, Potts. Just the same, we'll find out before anyone has to touch it, eh?'

Several of the men round about broke out in nervous chuckles. One of them enquired if the Lieutenant had made up his mind to go in over the wire, and Casson reminded him that they had only just set eyes on the target and that it was early days for him to decide anything definite.

While they were all lying prone and getting their breath back, a flying display was laid on for them which was totally unexpected. In from the north came four Stukas, flying in two pairs. They circled the airstrip, made contact with the ground staff and came in one at once with their flaps down and giving out a little of that peculiar noise which so terrified people who were going to be bombed or strafed by them.

They slowed in turn and taxied across the apron towards the fuel tanker and the alert crew which dealt with the refuelling and rearming. The perspex canopies were pushed back, and the flyers' heads appeared. Mostly they were grinning and talking and wiping their foreheads and faces where the goggles and helmets had made them perspire.

Corporal Johnson, the Liverpudlian, passed a remark which made several of the men think. 'You know, sir, if it wasn't for the German crosses an' their flag, you could almost think you were lookin' down on one of our fields!'

Casson nodded, and replied appropriately. He was about to look through his glasses again when he caught sight of Nick Burrows' face wrinkled in thought.

'Got any special ideas about the demolition, Burrows?'

'Yes, sir. If those four Stukas stay where they are all night, they'll constitute the main target for demolition. They'll have to go first. The buildings, fuel and that will have to take second place.'

Casson sounded disturbed. 'But you aren't advocating attacking the planes before the buildings and personnel, are you?'

Nick nodded very decidedly. 'That's exactly what I mean, sir. We ought to eliminate the kites first, then move in on the personnel.'

'But if you shoot up the planes, the personnel will have been alerted, and they will have a chance to fight back!'

Nick moved up the line, so that he was beside the subaltern.

'I figure now is as good a time as any for a discussion. I shall want to fix the planes by stealth, using incendiaries. While I'm working on the planes, you and most of the other men can be working your way into the field from another angle. Do you follow me?'

The temporary lines went out of the subaltern's brow. 'I think I do. The way you see this thing, we shall have a chance to get in and get at the Krauts before your demolition charges explode! Is that it?'

'That's it exactly, sir. I shall only require one man with me. Someone to help me negotiate the wire, and help me carry in the demolition stuff. My plan is to go under the wire, dig a shallow tunnel under it like the prisoners of war do. Once I've done my chore, I'll ghost across the field and join the rest of you.'

Knowing they were overheard by the whole unit, Casson spoke carefully. 'You are aware, of course, that your end of the business will not be easy. If, for instance, the sentry hears you scraping your hole under the wire, that might spring the alarm.'

Burrows nodded. 'I'm aware of that, sir. That's why I only want one man with me. If you've started about the same time as I do, you and the others will perhaps be inside the wire at a different point by then, and you'll still stand a chance of pulling off the operation in spite of the initial setback.'

Casson asked another couple of questions, offered one or two minor criticisms, and finally expressed himself as satisfied with Burrows' plan. He accepted it with a good grace, and secretly hoped that he would not have lost face with his men because the sapper had done most of the talking.

'Now, about this man you want to go with you. Do you want to ask for volunteers, or do you have someone in mind?'

Johnson cleared his throat. 'How about Ginger, sir? He's a good steady fellow, an' when he's not moanin' he can keep as quiet as anyone!'

Potts thanked the N.C.O. for the barbed compliment, and turned his eyes at once to get Burrows' reaction.

'If you could spare Private Potts, sir, I'd be very happy to have him along.'

Potts was so surprised that Burrows wanted him that all he could do was shrug and nod. For another half hour, details were thrashed out and then the men backed off their spur and prepared for a rather plain meal which did not involve the use of a fire. The small flat tins of action rations had long since ceased to interest men with appetites like theirs.

★   ★   ★

Exactly one hour after sunset, Nick Burrows and Ginger Potts crawled towards the airstrip perimeter wire near to the south-west corner. Everyone had been excited when the Stukas had been left in echelon formation just off the runway furthest west.

One bored-looking trooper in field grey, carrying a Schmeisser automatic pistol and the weight of the German war effort on his slightly stooped shoulders, moved disconsolately along the edge of the runway plucking the whiskers out of his rather fulsome nostrils and wondering just how absolutely stultifying a two-hour tour of duty could be on the most isolated German airstrip in the whole of Tunisia.

His jackboots on the concrete kept the intruders well informed of his movements and his whereabouts. Across towards the east, the hangers yawned in darkness. So did the guardhouse. Nobody expected trouble, apparently, this far off the beaten track.

The tarmac apron was conspicuously devoid of humans, and a turned up radio in the far block of offices, stores and billets seemed to suggest that everyone had gone off duty for the night, and were in that section. In the billets, the windows were open, and blackout curtains fluttered outwards, giving occasional flashes of light. Burrows remained as still as a lizard about ten yards from the wire.

'Well come on then, Nick,' Potts whispered, 'you've 'ad all your own way over this lark. When are we goin' to start? It's no good gettin' cold feet at this late stage, is it now?'

'Good grief, man, this is one of those occasions when you don't start moaning, not even if the ground opens up under you. All I wanted was to catch a glimpse of a Jerry over that side, that's all. I won't stop to explain why. I thought the sight of one loitering about would give us both confidence, that's all. Now then, let's go.'

They moved up to the fence, and cautiously started to scrape away the gritty soil from underneath it. Burrows gave up first. He moved ten yards further west, and called Potts to him. Potts was ready to rebel by this time, but when he realized that the soil in the second place was much easier to work, he decided against rebellion.

Although the passing of time jangled their nerves in the dark, and *Lily Marlene* on the radio seemed to go on endlessly, their hole under the fence took scarcely fifteen minutes to fashion.

Their faces were very close when the job of digging and scraping was done, and the German sentry, barely a hundred yards away, looked even less interested than before. 'Let me get ahead, and then follow through. I want to tackle the guard first, naturally. If anything goes wrong, try and wing him with your knife. Above all, keep it quiet whatever you do. All right?'

'I hope so, mate. I'd much rather be up the other end flankin' young Casson than actin' as rear guard for the likes of you!'

Nick frowned at him. 'Well, thanks for that vote of confidence, chum. I'll be off now.'

In the jumping smock he could have been mistaken for an outsize newt or lizard as he wriggled forward with arms and legs working. Soon, he was at the hole. His head ducked down with his trunk following. Behind him, Ginger Potts idly thought what he would have to do if Burrows was caught half way through the fence, but he soon gave up that form of mental exercise because it made his heart thump too hard.

Nick's boots disappeared and his head and shoulders came up on the inside. He was hauling along with him some of the small explosive charges with which he hoped to eliminate the Stukas. He wondered if anything would go wrong with the technical side of the business. This was no time to doubt his materials, though.

He unhooked the extras from his belt and went forward a little quicker, crossing the perimeter track, which was hard, in the least possible time. The sentry came towards the nearest plane just as he found his hands and knees back on hard grassy soil. It came as a relief to be able to rest and to see the German looking straight towards him without seeing anything untoward at all.

Even stripped to a Sten, he found his breath labouring as he crossed the last twenty yards towards the silhouettes of the planes. Heinrich, if that was his name, burped and moved away again, across the noses of the Stukas. Nick decided to follow him rather than wait for him to come back again another time. He thought the fellow might settle down at the other end.

He was right, too.

3

'Heinrich' was an expert secret smoker. He fished out a cigarette from a tin box and lit it, cupping his hand round the burning end with all the efficiency of a one-time civilian convict. He took his time about smoking it, too, resting his back against the wing roots of the fourth Stuka and drawing on it with satisfaction.

Nick kept right on, crawling on his belly underneath one plane after another. Weariness with this unaccustomed mode of travel slowed him up, and as the yards between him and the sentry dwindled, so the tension built up in him. He paused under the third plane, and loosened the knife which was fixed to his right calf.

If the fellow moved off now, at least he would have a chance of getting him by throwing the knife. He wriggled the last few yards, lowered his head on his forearms under the last kite and sucked in breath through his mouth. As casually as if in slow motion, the sentry shifted his shoulders, looked back towards the tail of the plane and suddenly threw back his head and opened his mouth.

Nick, who expected a shout to give the alarm, was caught on the hop. Seconds later, the guard yawned uninhibitedly and making no attempt to contain the noise he made. As he turned the other way again, Nick decided that his time had come. He gathered himself under the fuselage, and went forward at a crouched run.

One arm went round the fellow's throat, choking him, and, as the butt of the Schmeisser bounced off Nick's boot, the knife did its deadly work, sinking into the unprotected throat twice in rapid succession. Nick dropped the weapon behind him, point downwards in the dirt. He had not liked having to eliminate the fellow in cold blood, but the success of the whole strike depended on having him cold and out of the way.

Nick supported him, avoiding the blood which gushed from his neck. He undid the buttons of the tunic almost to the waist before lowering his victim to the ground.

'Ginger! Look out for my charges back there! Bring them along, an' hurry!'

Nick's voice was scarcely more than a whisper, but it sounded like a shout to a man as tensed up as he was.

'I've got 'em an' I'm nearly up with you, so nark it!'

'Keep on the ground till you get here. It won't do to show two figures instead of one.'

A minute later, Ginger Potts straightened up rather breathlessly beside the fourth plane. 'All right, I'm 'ere. Which planes do you want me to tackle? Oh, an' congratulations over what you did to the sentry. Looked good, what bit I could see.'

'Thanks, Ginger. I don't want you to touch the demolition stuff. I'll do that. Your job for the next few minutes is to be the sentry! Just borrow his helmet an' his tunic and parade up and down. And don't be long about it because his boots haven't hit the concrete in over five minutes!'

Potts rebelled and was told a few home

truths. Nick moved into the cockpit of the fourth Stuka in line and went to work with his demolition charges. They were designed to create a small explosion, after an interval which was preset, and then start a fire.

As he scrambled out of the first kite, he saw that Ginger was slowly pacing the concrete with the German helmet on his head. He had not bothered to put the grey tunic on.

'If anything goes wrong on account of your squeamishness, I'll murder you!' Nick promised.

'An' you'll be in your element tryin', but I wouldn't give much for your chances!'

'Have you forgotten your officer and the other blokes relying entirely on the outcome of this effort? What do you think will happen if somebody flashes a powerful torch across here an' sees that jumping smock?'

Nick scrambled into the second plane. His fingers were altogether steady by this time. He set a second charge for twenty minutes, and hoped that there would be no hold-ups once he had 'serviced' all the planes. When next he reached the ground, he noticed that Ginger was wearing the tunic, but with the neck open.

He decided to be tactful, for once in his life, and did not comment. 'Any sign of the others? Any Krauts knocking about?'

'Nothing at all, mate. Just us two, that German record programme, a lot of wasted light, an' a bombin' raid somewhere across there on the Med coast. We might be a couple of sentries in 'ell!'

Nick chuckled. He fixed a third plane, and then the fourth. By the time he was out of that one, his hands and arms were tired, and his legs ached through scrambling up and down. He leaned against a wing root and hoped he was invisible from the other side of the field. A curtain flapped in the lighted block. Nick flopped to the ground, and Ginger ambled towards him.

'All right, Field Marshal, what 'appens now?'

'As far as you're concerned, feldwebel, you stay here just walking up and down until the ruckus starts on the other side.

Then you can get across there just as fast as you like. Me, I'm going across there on my belly, just in case they have trouble.'

'Well, I'll go to 'ell!' Potts offered. ''Ave you thought what might 'appen if they suddenly decided to change the guard on this plane? Well, 'ave you?'

'I'm sorry, mate, but that's the way it has to be,' Nick reiterated. 'Keep things looking normal at this side until the ruckus starts. An' thanks for backin' me up!'

'An' what if the explosives go off before the ruckus starts, Mister Royal Engineer?'

Nick stiffened. It had not occurred to him that the strike over the other side might be so long delayed. 'Sorry, Ginger. If they haven't started in ten minutes, prop Heinrich up alongside a plane and come after me. An' don't forget to take his tunic off before you face up to our boys, eh?'

The sapper patted his partner's boot toe and set off across the concrete and grass towards the guard hut and the hangars. He was thinking ahead now to the other part of the operation. He thought Casson and the others might have shown themselves before this. There was something rather uncanny about the light and the music and the paras' non-appearance.

He longed for a few throaty blood-curdling yells to restore everything to rights. About seven or eight minutes had gone by when they came, and they made everything seem more unreal than before. Just when he was certain that something had delayed Casson's effort to get inside the perimeter wire, the subaltern and his corporal, followed by about half a dozen others, emerged like drab green ghosts from the open door of the hangar furthest to the north.

Already, they had looked into the guard hut, and the other hangars. Now, they were preparing to ghost across the mounded area which contained the air raid shelters and blast the personnel out of the extensive block beyond. Nick half rose on one knee, suddenly proud of the way the others were conducting themselves. He stayed quite still, like one of the lesser wild animals, with his senses working overtime for him.

The other men, about nine in number, emerged from the black mouth of the hangar and joined Casson. They ringed him cautiously and he gave them quiet orders. For about one hundred yards they kept together, and then, just as they were about to separate into small groups and attack the noisy block beyond, a heavy machine-gun, probably a Spandau, sounded off from the mouth of the nearest shelter.

Nick's body lurched, as though he had been hit. Like one hypnotized he saw the mouth of the weapon belching flame, and the tracers ripping across the pitifully few yards towards the green-smocked figures. Casson and three or four more men near him went down in the fashion of men who have absorbed bullets.

Others sprang about to face the new and unexpected menace. Still more threw themselves prone on the ground. But they were too late. From a second shelter, a small searchlight engulfed them. The first Spandau curtailed its burst, and another searchlight beam probed towards them. The paras were caught between two beams which paralysed their efforts for a few vital seconds. Afterwards, the survivors realized that delay might very well have saved their lives.

A scathing guttural voice barked an order at them. 'You *Englanders*! Drop your weapons! Stand up and raise your hands! *Schnell!* I give you three seconds!'

Somebody groaned very loudly. It was an expression of frustration rather than pain. A Liverpudlian voice said: 'Better do as Fritz says, lads, they've got us bang to rights!'

One after another, the green figures, bathed in bright light, rose to their feet, leaving their weapons on the ground. Out from the air raid shelters came the cock-a-hoop Germans, all carrying automatic weapons, mostly Schmeissers. They formed two pincers and closed a circle round the prisoners. As soon as the paratroops were ringed, their captors produced powerful hand torches and the searchlights were switched off.

Nick paused for several seconds, completely staggered by this unexpected reversal. Then he recovered himself and went forward again. He had to get into such a position that he could fire on the jubilant ring of guards without hitting the paras. It was not easy. He crawled and wriggled forward again, fearful that the Krauts might take his fellow countrymen off somewhere before he could take a hand. Obviously, the thing to do was to strike back before they got over their triumph.

At last, he thought he might try out his Sten. He threw himself flat again, wriggled another couple of yards and decided that if he fired high, all might be well. He was a little to one side of the Germans and he thought any bullets which missed would go skyward and miss the British. As an after-thought, he extracted from his pouch his two grenades. It would not do to mess up this chance of another reversal. His thoughts were busy with conjecture as to why he had got in unobserved if the Krauts had been expecting an attack. He touched the trigger rather lovingly and gritted his teeth. He squeezed, and panned his weapon round.

Grey clad men on the perimeter of the double group started to dance and throw themselves about. He counted four men killed for sure, and two more almost certain. Then he stopped his burst, and used his lungs.

'Red devils, hit the deck and come up shooting! You know where the enemy's located now! Go to it!'

With a roar of relief and gratitude those men who were still unscathed dropped to the ground. They stayed down and sprayed their oppressors with lethal doses of lead. For a few seconds it was Stens against Schmeissers at very close quarters. And then the first Spandau was in action again. The gunner had started firing before he had his weapon on a sufficiently low trajectory.

Bullets scythed in an arc over the paratroopers' heads as Nick hesitated between using his Sten, or throwing a grenade. Almost forgotten, the first of the Stukas erupted. It appeared to jump on its wheels. Its cockpit was enveloped in orange flame. A smaller secondary explosion occurred, and then the whole machine was burning like some huge cross. Its ammunition started to go up without warning.

Nick risked standing up. He pulled the pin of his first grenade and hurled it towards the shelter. It fell a couple of yards short, but was near enough to knock over the weapon and the man firing it. Then he was running, and working his way round behind the shelter.

He shouted: 'Hit 'em hard, lads! They're probably all here! And watch out for green smocks!'

A Schmeisser sent bullets after him as he ran. The weapon was fired from where the Spandau had been operating. It served to draw fire from one of the other paratroopers, and hostile fire died from that position.

A second Stuka became a torch, and then a third. In looking back, Nick saw an automatic weapon being fired from a position to the rear of the contestants, and further north than he had been. He deduced correctly that this was Potts making a strike.

He panted on and started to approach the mounded entrance of the second shelter from the rear. When he was ten yards away, a second Spandau opened up, shaking the ground underneath him. Bullets groped out across the darkness with Potts as their target. His gun went silent.

Nick sank to his knees. It was like being on a railway bridge over a cutting. He fought for breath, took time out to pull another pin, and dropped his grenade straight down into the sloping entrance of the shelter. This time, the explosion had the maximum effect. It demolished the gun and killed three men clustered round it.

Two other Germans of the original group to emerge fell before his Sten, and then he was walking forward to join the green smocks, who, thanks to the element of surprise, had succeeded in eliminating their captors.

Corporal Johnson identified Nick with a torch as they came together.

'Nice going, Burrows, you did a great job over there! We'll talk after. I want to crack this lighted block before we get caught again!'

'Thanks, Corp. Don't forget to look for the radio room first! I'll collect Ginger and we'll take a look at the casualties. After that, more demolition and then out, eh?'

Johnson approved. He waved his torch for the other men to join him. Nick shouted for Ginger, and to his great relief the other rose to his feet and trotted across to join him. They shook hands briefly. Nick pointed to the first of the shelters, which was still quiet.

'Drop a grenade in there, will you, Ginger, an' then come back and give me a hand!'

Uppermost in Potts' mind was the fate of his officer, but this time he fought down his rebelliousness and dropped the grenade into the other shelter from above. It killed two men who were crawling out with a view to doing some more fighting.

Potts hurried back and flopped down beside Nick, who had sorted out the casualties. The fourth Stuka went up unobserved. Nick gripped Potts' shoulder. 'I'm afraid your bloke has bought it, Ginger. I'm sorry. Three more blokes dead, too. The other one will patch up.'

Nick got to his feet and fumbled out an action wound dressing. Suddenly Ginger sprang up and came at him. The red-head had thumped him on the jaw before he knew what was happening, and he had gone down on his back with a jarring thud.

Pongo Smith, the wounded man, tutted gently.

Ginger said: 'You're a ruddy 'orrible bloke, Burrows! If you 'adn't picked me as your mate for that kite blowin' job, as like as not my bloke wouldn't 'ave died! I could 'ave protected 'im!'

Potts was almost sobbing. 'Take it easy, Ginger, we know how you must be feeling,' Pongo remarked quietly. He reached out and picked up the dressing which Nick had dropped. 'I don't think anybody could have helped him, chum. You see, that burst out of the bunker was too swift! Why don't you go off an' set fire to something? That'll make you feel better!'

Nick shook his head, rubbed his jaw and got to his knees. 'If I had the strength, I'd root out all the jeeps and such like, drive 'em onto the runways an' set fire to them!'

He clambered unsteadily to his feet, moved across to Smith and assisted with his wounds. One was on the outer side of his left upper arm, and the other was a gash on the top of his right shoulder. Potts started to recover himself almost at once. He had heard what Nick said, and he ran into the nearest hangar, hoping to atone for his recent misdeed.

He came out shortly afterwards driving a staff car, which he proceeded to pilot to the further runway.

'There's an oil tanker round the end of the far hangar,' Pongo remarked conversationally.

'Yes, I had noticed it,' Nick replied. 'I was hoping Ginger would leave that to me. A pity about all this — I mean about the Krauts rumbling us.'

Between them, Nick and Smith dragged the four bodies across to the slope between the bunker entrances. Meanwhile, the Stukas started to burn out, and the staff car took pride of place in the succession of conflagrations. Potts had burst the tank and dropped a match into the gushing petrol. He came racing back to the hangar as fast as his legs would carry him.

Johnson and the other fit men worked their way through the billets and offices, and, as Nick had suspected of late, all personnel had evacuated ready for the expected attack. They were never to find out the true reason for the Germans being warned. Actually, the Krauts were tipped off earlier by an Arab who had acquired a looted telescope. With this useful accessory, the native Tunisian had spotted the paras as they hiked across the hills earlier.

He had been rewarded by the airstrip C.O.

Smith went along with Nick to the tanker. They mounted up in the cab and drove off with it. First they circled the guard house, then it was in and out of the hangars, and all the time the feed hose was leaking aviation fuel. Finally, they put a combustible border round the billets and offices, and the green smocks threw into the fuel anything that easily came to hand.

Johnson had the honour of igniting the fuel. He did this just as Potts fired a second jeep on the other runway. As fire licked along the trail of ignited fuel, the corporal called his men together and gave them brief orders for evacuating the airstrip.

The night had been a success, after all, but they wanted to survive to join the main party. Burdened as they were with the bodies of four of their comrades, the withdrawal was slow. Fortune, however, enabled them to move a few hundred yards beyond the perimeter wire and blend in with the darkened countryside before other Axis units appeared.

By that time, the ringed billets and offices were disintegrating within the flaming moat, which was consuming everything.

Two German reconnaissance aircraft, flying down from the north, had a telling view of the damage from a high altitude. It was sad tidings they took back with them; tidings which kindled anger against the green warriors who had dropped from the skies.

4

Some four miles away from the German airstrip, the weary paratroopers found a niche for themselves in a gully between steep-sided hills. It was away from the only road in the area and well wide of the nearest track. Lieutenant Casson and the other three dead were laid out in line away from the rest of the men.

A digging detail turned out at dawn and at once commenced to dig a communal grave for the three troopers and a separate one about a yard away for the officer. No thought was given to breakfast until the graves were prepared and the whole outfit had mustered to give their dead comrades the best possible send off.

Corporal Johnson was out of his element acting as padre, but he did his best, reciting an odd line or two of the burial service, expressing the thoughts of all present and concluding with part of a psalm. He stepped back rather lamely when he had finished and saluted. At a nod, the rest fell out, and permission was at once given to rustle up food.

Two fires were lit. Four capable men took charge of the cooking and others moved out to east and west, and up the nearest hill slope to make sure they were not surprised, or overlooked without their knowledge. The surprise reception which the German ground staff had given them at the airstrip served to make them one of the most vigilant of units for as long as they survived.

Fifteen men plodded away from the site of the burial and the camp. One N.C.O., namely Corporal Johnson; one wounded man, Pongo Smith; one trained sapper, Nick Burrows, and twelve others. Although a mere forty hours or so had elapsed since they jumped, their packs were now appreciably lighter. Tinned stores, for instance, had gone down. So had the number of spare magazines for their Stens. And the demolition charges used on the Stukas, as well.

This lessening of the load put a spring

in the step of men who otherwise would have been sluggish, having regard for the number of miles which they had already covered on foot and the fighting of the night before.

Ginger Potts led the column with Corporal Johnson close behind him. It was not that the Liverpudlian felt the need for an advance guard. Since he had assumed command of the small outfit, he knew a compulsion to refer to the maps fairly frequently. And a man at the head of a column who kept looking down at maps was scarcely the type for a forward lookout.

Samuel Crosby Johnson, known to his cronies as Scouse, frequently removed his headgear and ran his fingers through his thinning hair. Those who followed behind took note that even Scouse had moments when he needed to reread. In other words, he was human and he was taking the job very seriously.

Nick Burrows was the back marker. At breakfast, he had endured a lot of good natured chaffing from the survivors. Mostly it had to do with his having penetrated the field as far as the planes without having been spotted by Krauts who had already been alerted. Some said he moved like a fairy, and others claimed he had eyes in his posterior.

For once, Nick had grinned and blushed, and agreed to bring up the rear on account of his having eyes in his rear portion.

As the morning progressed, the gully down which they were walking gradually widened out. As the hills receded on either side, the men became jumpy for a while. Here and there, rugged mountain sheep appeared and every man of his own accord looked for the shepherd without success. The sun, though far less strong than it had been in the summer months, shone down on their backs and dried out the chunky soil beneath their feet.

For a time, the going became easier. The muddy soil lost its excess moisture. But subsequently, the drying soil became dusty and more like sand in texture. So, as the booted feet gradually tired, the softer going tended to hold them back. Water bottles were frequently used, and the perspiration dried out on their clothing not long after it had formed.

Nick recollected from talks they had been given prior to leaving Algiers that the weather in Tunisia was likely to deteriorate very decidedly before the end of the year. He wondered what the Allies' chances were of stamping out all opposition in Tunisia before Christmas.

This far, the British had been on the receiving end of the stick for so long that neither he nor any of his comrades would have gambled when the world conflict might end.

'*Down men!*'

Nick dropped to the ground with great alacrity, and yet he was one of the last to take the weight off his feet. A few seconds before the barked command, Johnson had waved his arm through a half circle to indicate an unexpected halt. Nick peered round behind him rather guiltily, and yet he felt reasonably sure that no one had come along in their rear unnoticed.

Almost at once, the sounds which had caused the stir at the front of the column carried down the whole of the line.

Engines! They sounded like powerful motor cycle engines coming directly towards them at a slow speed.

Every man knew that they would either have to give a good account of themselves or be hidden by the time the strangers arrived.

Nick glanced round him, his heart thumping. The talus rocks at the foot of the slope on the south side were the nearest, but there was a separate rock cluster beside an upthrusting pinnacle of rock some seventy yards to the north. This cluster afforded the closest cover, but if they had to evacuate from there, the foot of the northern slope was as far away again.

Nick was doubtful about using the rock cluster, but he knew this was not his decision. Neither could he see as well as those up the front.

Johnson came up on one knee and pointed to the rock cluster. Another gesture brought every man up from the ground and haring across the seventy yards as fast as his aching limbs would carry him. Nick was one of the last three in cover. He dived on the ground, rolled onto his back, and panted for breath.

Johnson and Potts each had out a pair of glasses which they were putting to good use.

The word went from man to man. 'Motor cycle combinations. Jerries on some sort of patrol. Three men to each combo. They don't appear to have seen us. Orders are to keep quiet and lie low.'

Nick turned to Pongo Smith, who was fairly fresh because he had not been required to carry a heavy pack. 'Here, Pongo, do you reckon they're looking for us in particular?'

'I dare say, Nick. After all, we did all the damage, didn't we? I wouldn't think we're out of trouble when they've gone past either, because we're a bit off the beaten track here. We may meet up with this shower again before we link up with the main party.'

'I only hope Johnson has a clear idea as to where the rendezvous is,' Nick remarked.

A man made a noise which was almost a faint whistle. Those who were not actively peering out of the cluster of rocks stiffened, and strained their ears. One or more of the combinations had stopped. Men pulled their heads in still further and signalled for their friends to crouch even lower.

There were three motor cycle combos altogether, and their senior N.C.O. had chosen this particular location to stop for a ten minute rest. All three bikes stopped. The men swarmed out of them. Surprisingly, two men trotted across the open ground to the near side of the rock pinnacle and there they started to answer the call of nature while they talked to one another in loud voices.

The paras turned their heads and frowned at one another. They could visualize other considerations which might bring a modest German round the back. When all the paras were perspiring, the feldwebel called to the men who were now propping up the pinnacle.

Grumbling quietly to themselves, they moved back to the combinations and one of them produced matches to light cigarettes. A long five minutes went by after that before the crews finally scrambled back into their machines and drove off towards the west. The paras stayed where they were. Some smoked, others talked and some moistened the rear side of the rock pinnacle.

When they were ready to move on again, Johnson remarked: 'As things turned out we outnumbered that little mob, but I didn't attack them because even if we wiped them out we'd only bring more searchers on our tracks an' we haven't rejoined our main party yet.'

Nobody offered any comment. On they went again, looking for a track over higher ground which would not leave them so vulnerable in the event of motorized searchers coming up quickly. Before they found the track they sought a prowling Junkers tested the speed with which they could get into effective cover, but again, they remained undetected.

★   ★   ★

Major Dunstable and the main column of paratroopers were only a few miles away

68

from the airstrip party. They had with them a few mules, two small carts and a trolley. This should have made them speedier over the ground, but on countless occasions they had been frustrated by prowling Germans who could have brought them serious trouble before the important tank harbour was reached.

The day after Johnson's men had narrowly avoided the motor cyclists the main column was moving along a meandering hill track on the south side of a valley some ten miles further east. They had kept going for a few miles during the dark hours of the previous night because the landscape was beginning to level itself out and they were not sure about how well hidden they would be when the sun rose.

A handful of the best lookouts were on the alert when the sun came up that morning. They trained their glasses on an Arab farm situated a little over half a mile to the north-east. Upwards of a dozen labourers surged out of the house at an early hour and went to work in the crops and the plantation of olives. Others

69

started to milk rather ribby cows out at the back. A couple of nanny goats gave up milk, too.

Dunstable was of the opinion that the native Arab was a doubtful customer. He supposed a native could not be blamed for not showing loyalty to an invader, even if the invader claimed to have come along to put out a previous invader.

The Major decided that his outfit was safe just so long as they did not light fires. While the men fed themselves the best they could on cold food and drink, the C.O. went into a huddle with his officers about how they were going to get down off the heights, or, alternatively, how they were going to bypass the farm without giving away their position.

Several officers spoke, and when the Major took his turn, he advocated extreme caution.

'In my opinion the best way to sound out that farmer — if we make contact at all — is to slip a handful of men away from here and have them approach the farm from a different direction.'

The discussion progressed, and within

minutes all had agreed that the Major's plan best suited their present needs. If a small party met with unfriendliness or hostility, the rest of the outfit could remain safe.

Accordingly, a sergeant and six troopers slipped away from the camp site and began a wide detour so as to come upon the farm from the north. They had progressed scarcely more than half a mile when a growing cloud of dust started to approach from eastward. The watchers were filled with apprehension, especially when it was seen that this was German armour. No less than eight Tiger tanks pulled up opposite the farm, and labourers surged out of it to help the crews fill their water bottles from a well in the yard.

The tank crews stayed by the farm for a good half hour before moving on towards the west in an unhurried dusty column. The recce party almost called off their excursion, but the will of the N.C.O. prevailed, and in the early afternoon they tramped towards the northern boundary of the establishment where an old man, and a fatter younger one who might have been his son, worked to turn the stubborn soil with the assistance of an ox and a donkey.

This pair seemed friendly enough, and gradually the party came round to the idea that the British would be well received. They went indoors, and talked to the farmer himself. An hour before sunset, a signaller with the recce party flashed a message.

The gist of it was as follows: *The farmer and his family are prepared to take in and feed all the British personnel provided they wait until after dark before showing themselves.*

The C.O. sent back a brief reply which suggested that they were glad to accept the offer. A half hour after sunset, the paras left their hill slope and were absorbed into the farm where their nostrils caught the aroma of *cous-cous*, a kind of meat stew which could be produced on a large scale.

★　★　★

By eleven o'clock the following morning, the party from the airstrip found themselves in exactly the same position which the larger party had occupied before descending on the farm. Johnson's party ferreted around the camping site and turned up very definite signs which led them to believe the other party had passed that way quite recently.

The farm opposite looked innocent enough for its occupants to know nothing of prowling paratroops, and yet one could never be quite sure. If they failed altogether to make contact with the main party, Johnson was determined that they would not walk into an ambush.

He decided to wait and to watch. No squadron of tanks approached to alleviate boredom, but a familiar sound came along from westward a little after midday. The motor cycle combinations were on the prowl again! They bumped and bounced along a poorly surfaced road, and made a left turn towards the north about half a mile short of the farm.

The road ran north for perhaps another half mile, and then turned north-east and ran off out of sight, presumably towards the Gulf of Hammamet or the Gulf of Tunis further north.

No sooner had the combination crews made the north turn than two Arabs detached themselves from the plough working in the rear of the farm and scampered soundlessly across land to intercept the Kraut patrol. Johnson and all the men with him immediately thought of treachery.

'We should have blasted that outfit when we had the chance before,' the Corporal muttered bitterly.

'Let's get down onto lower ground,' Nick begged anxiously. 'We're too far off to challenge them here!'

Potts joined in a three-man discussion as to where they should go as soon as they were sure the motor cycle patrol would come back.

'I figure we ought to position ourselves right below here so we can threaten them when they use this farm approach track,' Johnson opined.

'Mines are what we need this time!' Nick enjoined. 'The obvious place would be a few yards up that northbound stretch of road, but I don't think I could get there in time!'

'But you could get down there on this track,' Johnson persisted. 'We'll all try to get down unobserved as soon as they show signs of returning.'

Nick wanted to put his mines beyond the road intersection, further to westward, but he perceived that a prolonged argument might spoil their chances of a successful strike.

'They've stopped,' Potts shouted. 'And what's more the Wogs are talking to them like long lost brothers. The rearmost combo is turning round!'

'They aren't coming straight back, though,' Nick argued. He wanted time to get his mines set up.

While Johnson was snapping his fingers to draw the men together, the sapper asked Pongo Smith to help him carry one or two mines down to the lower level. Within a minute, the paratroopers were slipping down the slope and taking advantage of every possible bit of cover.

Nick, apparently as contrary as ever,

insisted on moving further west along the track with Pongo before coming down off the heights. Johnson, glancing back, saw what he was doing. He murmured: 'If Burrows beggars this up, I'll have him for it.'

5

After that, it was all scrambling, crouching and staring.

Twelve men went down the obvious way behind Scouse Johnson. They had to watch carefully where they put their feet, and at other times their questing eyes roved between the farm, the combinations and the informers, and the rutted track below them which was their destination.

Burrows and Smith drew steadily further away from the others until Smith became breathless and started to drop behind.

'Ain't it time we were getting down below now, Nick?' he panted. 'We're almost opposite the intersection, and the rest are way below us!'

'Just another few yards, then down we go,' Nick promised.

Smith laboured on at a distinct disadvantage with his awkward shoulder and arm wounds. He perceived that Nick had something in mind which did not altogether tie in with what Johnson had intended. He hoped that whatever it was, it came off, and proved itself worthwhile.

Nick was afraid that the talking Germans, who were digesting more and more details of intelligence, might look directly back up their road and see two scrambling paratroopers coming down towards them. That was why he insisted on going past the intersection. At last, he was satisfied.

He came to a halt on one knee, took some more of the weight off his assistant, and started down the slope. 'If you get a bit behind, Pongo, don't let it bother you. I've got plenty to do once I get down there!'

Nick was every bit as observant as the others had been when he began his descent. He found himself going over and over in his mind his reasons for acting in the way he was doing. Being the only sapper, he saw it as his responsibility that mines should be planted at the most strategic places. He hoped he was not letting himself down, apart from the Corporal, with the weight of responsibility he carried.

Smith was obsessed with the idea that the Germans or the Arabs must see them before they reached the road. Rather miraculously, the attention of both parties appeared to be held elsewhere. The wounded man lurched onto flat ground and at once took time out to see how his mates had gone on.

Even as he looked, the last pair threw themselves down prone behind low rock and scrub a few yards back from the farm track. They looked to be about a hundred yards on the farm side of the intersection.

'Buck up, Pongo,' Nick called, having reached a point beside the road.

He was kneeling down, giving his full attention to three mines which, in ordinary circumstances, would have been buried a little way under the soft surface of the road. Now, there was no time for that. He saw to the priming, and took from Pongo a length of cord. This he used to link the three mines with about a yard between them.

'They're starting to come back, Nick,' Pongo ejaculated.

He was blinking his heavy-lidded eyes and betraying great excitement. Nick wondered if his wounds had left him with a touch of fever.

'All right, Pongo, I'm about ready. As you must have guessed, *I* think the Krauts will come this way, see. I'm going to nip across with the rest of this cord in a minute. Then I'll pull the mines slowly into the middle of the road. Anything you can do towards covering them with light dirt will help. If the combinations keep rolling, I can haul on the cord when they're right under the wheels. If anything goes wrong, use your loaf, mate. And thanks for helping!'

Pongo answered that it was a pleasure, and felt sure that Nick would not believe him. Nick flashed him a rare crooked smile, and darted across the road almost bent double. With a good quarter inch of blue-black beard on his chin, he looked wilder than ever before.

Nick reached the other side of the road and dived into the scrub. He sneezed on fine dust and at once started to haul the mines away from Smith and towards him. When they were across the middle section of road, he stopped pulling and signalled for Smith to throw dirt on them.

The combinations were thundering steadily nearer, but they still had a minute or two in hand. Gradually the telltale metal containers were transformed into brown mounds not unlike mole hills in miniature.

★ ★ ★

The first of the motor cycle combinations rocked and rumbled towards the turn in the road. Holding the handlebars was a lantern-jawed trooper with a protruding underlip. Seated in the sidecar was a fleshy man who perspired a lot in the confines of his seat. His head jolted from side to side directly behind the rear end of a Spandau machine-gun mounted on the front of the sidecar.

The feldwebel in charge of the patrol was seated on the pillion behind the driver nursing his Schmeisser. His wide

81

thin-lipped mouth was spread in a triumphant grin as he considered what he had heard from the lips of the accommodating old Arab and his son. Hundreds of *Englander* paratroops hiding within the confines of the farmhouse and its outbuildings. Probably the men who had set fire to the airstrip on the road to Pont du Fahs! Too much for nine tired motor cycle troopers to tackle, but a squadron of tanks would make mincemeat out of them. And some of the credit for the victory would have to go to him because he had been the man to acquire the intelligence.

His grin broadened even more as another thought occurred to him. Why shouldn't the combinations return after the tanks? The Panzers could cope all right, but no doubt a few of the paratroopers would try and escape across country. And they would be easy victims on the run!

In a way, he was glad that his radio was kaput. It gave him a chance to get well clear of the danger zone until the Panzers arrived.

He was so pleased with himself that he almost fell off the pillion as the driver made the right turn. He was wondering whether he should give the informers a packet of cigarettes as a reward at a later date when two loose mounds of dust appeared to disintegrate just ahead of them.

The driver cried: '*Gott im Himmel!* What sort of animals do they have in these places? The moles make dust screens?'

Before anyone else could comment, the first mine exploded directly under the front wheel of the bike. There was an ear-splitting crash, an upward flying cone of explosive, and the front wheel, fork and handelbars appeared to rise in the air and disintegrate at the same time. Needless to say, the unfortunate driver was killed instantly. His pulverized corpse was thrown a great distance away. At the same time, the feldwebel was thrown backwards with several fragments of steel deeply buried in his body. A mere two or three seconds later, a second mine exploded under the sidecar and the elimination of the first outfit was complete.

A small amount of twisted metal and a part of a tyre continued to burn across the small oval-shaped double crater as the second combination rolled towards the scene. The driver of the second outfit appeared to be staring sightlessly at the heap of burning wreckage, while his sidecar passenger couldn't take his eyes from a spinning helmet which was all that was left of his opposite number up ahead.

Nick Burrows' Sten was a few seconds slower in going into action than that of Pongo Smith. The latter knew that he would not be able to control his weapon long with one hand. He squeezed a burst at the nearest enemy, the man in the second sidecar. He was accurate for long enough to kill the man behind the Spandau.

Nick accounted for the driver and pillion rider in one panned burst. The second outfit ran into the crater and fouled itself up. Meanwhile, the third driver pulled up short. His sidecar passenger was aiming the Spandau towards Smith's hideout spot when more hostile fire came from directly to the rear.

Johnson, Potts and two others had stepped into the track, just beyond the intersection. Two of them were firing Bren guns from the hip, and the other pair used their Stens. Within another thirty seconds, the action was over. Every German was dead.

Nick and Pongo walked round the crater and met their friends by the third combination. The Corporal pointed a long horny forefinger at Nick's chest. 'And don't start to tell me you thought I wanted the mines planted beyond this intersection, because your excuse won't wash! You're an awkward devil, Burrows, an' I'm beginning to know you better than a brother!'

He rubbed a finger across his face under the Roman nose and suddenly grinned. 'But ye gods, you sure are deadly when it comes to getting rid of Jerry! The Major and the others back there will be wondering what on earth has been happening — if they're at the farm!'

'I'm sorry if I mugged you about,

Corp,' Nick answered soberly. 'Since that little lot went up, I'm beginning to wonder if we ever needed the mines. We could have stopped Jerry just as well without and still had our mines in hand.'

Johnson pretended to do a mock faint. Several willing hands caught him. 'Now he tells us,' Johnson murmured, as Potts fanned his face with a para's veil. 'I've a good mind to put him on a charge! That would shake him.'

'Anybody see where the informers went to?' Pongo asked conversationally.

'Yer, *I* saw 'em,' Potts replied, stabbing his own chest with his forefinger. 'They doubled straight back over to that ploughed field, as though nothing had happened. Now there's a thing, Corp. 'Ow about letting me sort out those two Wogs? Nothing would give me greater pleasure than to 'ave their guts for garters!'

Johnson suddenly turned serious. 'We've got to make contact with the other boys and get them to move out in double quick time! Otherwise we'll all be in dead trouble!'

'Somebody's flashing an identification signal from a farm window,' Potts informed them excitedly. 'Usin' a torch, I shouldn't wonder!'

'Then they must 'ave guessed it's us!' Johnson decided.

He called to his signaller and told him to stand by with a message. While the signaller and Johnson primed the party in the farm with the latest information, Nick and Pongo succeeded in turning the third of the combinations around. Nick took the controls and Pongo clambered into the sidecar. Potts won the race for the pillion seat, and the rest of the men walked alongside of the outfit.

Pongo held up his head-gear on the end of his Sten as the motor cycle took them slowly down the track to the farm entrance. More Arabs had swarmed out, and looks of amazement at the German reversal were changing to expressions suitable for welcome.

Potts leaned across to the Spandau.

'By rights, I reckon the two Arabs who ratted on our outfit ought to be put in front of that gun and mown down.'

He said this in all seriousness without any thought of dramatizing the event, and several men were in full agreement. The morse message, however, put the initiative into the hands of those warriors already in the farm.

Major Dunstable himself checked the details of the message. He walked out at the back of the farm with his second in command and marched the two offending Arabs out of the ploughed field. When they saw the looks on the faces of the paratroopers, they started to protest and gesticulate.

Dunstable's face was white and drawn. He managed to hold himself in until the motor cycle combination arrived. Nick, Pongo and Ginger all identified the informers beyond any doubt.

Potts thought back to the airstrip, and the deaths of Casson and the others. There must have been an informer or informers on that occasion. The trooper drew himself up smartly.

'Sir, I'd like to be one of the firing squad which deals with these men!'

Dunstable nodded. Five other men

who had been to the airstrip joined the redhead. Very solemnly, the protesting Arabs were manhandled out of the back door of the farm and placed against a wall. They were given blindfolds. The farmer and others, who protested, were violently thrown aside.

The Major raised and lowered his arm. The automatic weapons juddered briefly. The bodies were hurled about. They fell and lay still.

Dunstable's interpreter told the farmer to have the bodies buried, and to take warning about what had happened. Then, and only then, men who had been separated since shortly after the jump came together and threw their arms around one another.

Details of the clash at the airstrip were bandied about.

Dunstable finally cut short the joyful reunion, and reminded all present that they would have to be on their way in a very short time.

'Talk and smoke, if you want to, but be ready to move off at very short notice.'

So saying, he retired into another room

with his second in command, and at once sent for Corporal Johnson and Nick Burrows to hear a more detailed report. As he listened, the Major wished he had taken part in the minor strike.

Soon, the four stood up and the order went round to stand to.

6

As a further lesson to the Arabs for their countrymen's treachery the farmer and his labourers were brought away from the burial and made to manhandle the carts, the trolley and the sound motor cycle combination across the ploughed land at the back of the buildings as far as the road which went off to the north-east.

At a word from their officers, the paratroopers stepped clear of cover and hurried along behind the vehicles. Soon, the whole outfit was assembled on the road and Dunstable waved to set them walking forward. Their steps were brisk as they moved away from the danger area four abreast. There was no need to appoint men as lookouts, because every mother's son had decided that his eyes would not be the last to see trouble, in the event that it came looking for them.

Already, most of the details of what had happened to Casson's outfit were known to the main party. Troopers who envied the small troop their run of good luck often glanced towards the motor cycle combination with looks of unbounded admiration.

Nick, Pongo and Ginger Potts had resumed their earlier places on it and in it, and nobody seemed to begrudge them the honour, although Dunstable and his second-in-command were striding along not many yards in front.

Corporal Johnson had joined the officers and the other men of his troop were tagging along behind the German machine.

Johnson seemed anxious, and soon the discussion of the strike against the airstrip was suspended until the officers found what he had in mind.

'Sir, I'd like to put forward a suggestion, if I may.'

Dunstable quirked an eyebrow at his second-in-command and nodded for Johnson to proceed. The C.O. was thinking that this man's army had a lot to be said for it when its corporals had definite ideas on how it should be run.

'Sir, some time in the near future, this outfit is going to get a hell of a pasting when Jerry catches up with it. That, of course, has to be avoided, if possible, especially as the main attack has not been carried out yet. I was thinking that if a small party made a diversion, drew the enemy forces in the wrong direction as soon as they appeared, then the main party would stand a much better chance of survival and ultimate success.'

Johnson paused for breath. A smile flickered over his hard features. It went faster than it came and left him feeling extremely embarrassed between the two officers.

'Do go on, Corporal,' Dunstable suggested. 'I think I know where your thoughts are taking you, but we'll have to have a few details, don't you think?'

'Thank you, sir. I'd say you ought to slope off with all the personnel which was at the farm as soon as some worthwhile cover shows itself towards the south-east. You ought to leave with us, that's Lieutenant Casson's troop, the combination and the carts, plus the trolley. Not because we want to use them especially, but because havin' them along with us will give us a better chance of foxin' pursuit. Do I make myself clear, sir?'

'Amply, Johnson. We've listened most carefully, and I think your plan is quite sound. I'll take the main party directly towards the tank harbour and your outfit can draw off opposition and endeavour to join us in time for the strike. Have you got your map handy?'

Johnson produced his rather grubby plan of the area and hastily unfolded it. Dunstable, assisted by the other officer, indicated as near as possible the exact location of the farm which they had just left. He pointed out afresh where the tank harbour and workshop was, and estimated when his party might be in a position, to make the strike.

Johnson listened with rapt attention, mouthing the details silently. Dunstable gave him ample time to ask about anything which was not clear. Quite suddenly the C.O. chuckled. He flicked up the ends of his moustache which appeared to have lost dignity since his chin bristles grew.

'All right then, we'll take that as settled. You drop back an' brief your boys, and we'll see about making up deficiencies of stores and ammunition.'

This time, the Corporal's smile was broader. 'Many thanks, sir. It's mostly basic stuff we'll need. Food, Sten magazines, grenades, an' mines.'

He saluted, and stepped back into the path of the combination. Nick, who had been watching the discussion up front with interest, slowed a little and drove alongside of him. The walking members of the troop shuffled closer, chewing on gum and trying to read the expression on Johnson's face.

'You're goin' to 'ate me before this jaunt's over, lads. I've just asked for you to take on another isolated an' difficult assignment. The rest of the boys are goin' to leave us quite soon. We're going to soldier on an' try an' take any pursuin' Krauts along with us! In a minute, I want two of you to take on as drivers of the carts.'

'Just one thing, Corp!' Potts called. 'I

'ope you've laid it on for us all to 'ave a decoration if we come out of this lot? I mean we don't want the old chest to look too bare when we fall in with the rest of the British Legion, do we?'

Men on all sides suggested that Ginger should nark it, which he promptly did. Johnson cut short the details of what he wanted to pass on, and contented himself with watching the transfer of excess stores from the carts to the backs of men.

Messengers came to the front of the line. They were told what to say to all officers and N.C.O.s and as they passed back, so the news of the coming split was received by everyone down to ordinary troopers. A buzz of excitement went through the ranks. The sky and the road to the rear grew less interesting. Instead, many pairs of eyes peered ahead, looking for the likeliest place to turn off.

Actually, a mile and a half had gone by, and the farm was well to the rear, when Dunstable spotted a big oval patch of camel thorn scrub and stunted desert trees. In all, the area was about the size of a large football pitch. He thought this would have to do, in the absence of other screening material.

The two officers in the lead stepped to one side. A special arm signal caused the men who were going off the road to step to do the same. The men who had been driving the carts this far shook hands with their reliefs and sprang to the ground. Suddenly, Johnson's outfit spread over the combination, two carts, and a trolley seemed pitifully small.

Every man still on the road raised his arm in friendly salute as the remainder jumped a shallow ditch and went towards the timbered copse. Nick, at the controls of the big motor cycle, shuddered without knowing quite why.

'How about speeding up a bit, Corp? I don't want to bother you, but if the Jerries come looking for us in a hurry they'll blast us right off the face of the earth! What we want is a place we can run for in the event we're spotted!'

'All right, you don't 'ave to tell me, Burrows! I'd 'ave given the order before this only I didn't want it to look like a rout to the blokes who've just taken cover!'

Johnson scrambled aboard the first of the carts. Every other man did the same except two who were pulling a trolley. A half hour went by, during which they traversed almost three miles of the bumpy road. The Corporal anxiously surveyed the road ahead through glasses. At last he saw a greenish clump which took some of the lines out of his forehead.

He jumped to the ground, and ran to overtake the combination, using the pillion seat vacated when Potts decided to be a mule coaxer.

''Ere, Pongo, take a look and see what you think!'

The wounded man in the sidecar was quick to oblige. 'Sure, we could hide there, Corp. I suppose you don't want to unless something comes after us, though. We'll have to play this like musical chairs. Go slowly towards that clump an' then accelerate afterwards.'

Johnson looked at Smith in amazement, and all he could do was nod.

Nick increased his revs, and the mules bringing up the carts speeded up behind him. Soon, the two men pulling the trolley shouted for a let up in speed. They called in vain. One of them measured the increasing distance between themselves and the nearer of the two carts in front. He then glanced back, and a tiny speck in the sky not much bigger than an eyelash engaged his attention. He tapped his partner on the shoulder and pointed back.

Lofty Wright, a Mancunian with prominent teeth, at once spotted the cause of his partner's alarm. He was startled enough to lose his chewing gum down the back of his throat.

'Hell's bells, a fighter, Jock! *One of theirs!*'

The fighter, small in the sky behind them, was indeed a German. Its pilot was searching for signs of the trio of combinations which were overdue in communicating with their base.

Wright cupped a hand to his mouth and bellowed a warning. He had to repeat it before it was heard on account of the mules' hooves and the sound of the motor cycle engine. Pongo pulled out the German helmet which he had picked up for a souvenir. He stuck it on his head.

Johnson waved the whole outfit forward again. 'We should all have had Jerry helmets, that way the pilot might have hesitated!'

Unfortunately for the fleeing airborne soldiers the Messerschmitt quickly located the place where the first combination had been blown up. From there it did not take long to follow the road and to see signs of activity. The pilot sent it over the road at scarcely more than two hundred feet. A certain amount of dust had been put up by the animals, carts and combination, and as he roared over the first time his machine-guns were quiet and his eyes busy.

Nick drew the combination aside a yard or two short of tree cover. Johnson waved the carts and the trolley forward with an impatient gesture. Just as the Messerschmitt raced by overhead, Pongo Smith stood up in his sidecar and waved. He was the only man with a German helmet and his wave drew the pilot's attention towards him for perhaps a second.

The plane zoomed on, made a climbing

turn and started to come back again. By that time, the combination had been coaxed a few yards into timber, and everyone felt better for the cover however inadequate it was.

The pilot circled the trees, obviously far from satisfied. Finally, he came in quite low and cut loose with his machine-guns. Bullets scythed their way through the foliage and the tree boles sending men diving in all directions.

'Everybody down low and start digging!' Johnson bellowed.

By now, everyone knew the enormity of the task which they had taken on. The German army was strong in northern and eastern Tunisia and since the First Army's strike in the west, the *Luftwaffe* strength had been built up with squadrons flown across from Sicily.

The paratroopers began to think that they had been extremely lucky on the day of their jump. Out came the shovels and the earth began to fly. The fighter pilot came at them twice more. Good luck more than anything else preserved the diminutive outfit before he pulled away.

Men stuck their fingers in their ears and swallowed to clear them as the sky grew quiet again. Nick broke off in his digging and walked to the northern boundary. He borrowed a pair of glasses and trained them towards the north-east. Johnson joined him, doing the same.

'After this, if we survive, the nearest high ground appears to be about five miles away,' Nick muttered. 'I wonder if they'll give us the chance to get up there, ever?'

'Might as well look on the bright side, chum,' Johnson remarked. 'After all, we've been fairly lucky so far.'

Nick glared at him, and went back to his digging. Fifteen minutes later, two Stukas came probing their position. Nobody needed to be told to take cover as the first of them slipped into its dive and the nerve-shattering roar came from it. The paratroopers dived into their slit trenches like frogs too long out of water.

Small shells pierced the copse along a wide swath, but two Bren guns answered as the pilot pulled out and the plane showed its underbelly. Tracers chased it for several seconds and then the second marauder with the bent wings was screaming on its way down. This one came at a different angle so that its cannon shells ravaged a second swath which made a cross with the first.

Miraculously, only two superficial cuts were inflicted during these two attacks, and those came from flying pieces of metal. The attackers had obviously been given very definite instructions about what was to be done if the enemy was sighted.

In its second dive, the first Stuka detached a small bomb which tumbled over and over, flashing in the sun.

'No more shooting after this bomb lands!' Johnson shouted hoarsely.

Men whose heads and shoulders were pressed to the earth wondered what idea had prompted such a remark. Even Nick Burrows was not at all sure. That day, the bomb aimer was on form. His small bomb sailed down on a straightening parabola and finally landed plumb in the middle of the copse. The whole of the timbered area lurched as though it was somehow detached from the rest of the earth. Two trees were demolished. Earth and roots flew upwards in an inverted cone, covering the two carts and showering the combination.

Those men whose slit trenches had been partially filled up by the soil and debris shook themselves free and cautiously peered above the surface. They were in time to see Corporal Johnson scramble to his feet and point to the new pit.

'Everybody into the crater, as fast as you like! Come on, now, chop, chop!'

The copse suddenly came to life and men dived into the new hollow from all sides. Johnson, himself, was the last man into the pit. He put a knee in a man's stomach and took time out to apologize.

''Ere comes Number Two! Now, everybody spread out an' look dead, see? Make it look real!'

Nick had his doubts as to whether the pilots could see into the bottom of the bit, but he appreciated the good sense behind the Corporal's idea. The next bomb was five yards wide of the copse, and several of the troop shook with the laughter of relief when the immediate tension was over.

Another diving attack was made by one plane, using cannon shells again, and finally the avenging pair pulled away and headed back for the north. The personnel crawled out of the pit and looked round them, but stayed in the trees. Although two or three more cuts and bruises had been sustained every man pronounced himself fit to carry on as before. The mules had taken a shaking, but they, too, were fit for further service. Lofty Wright scrambled up a tree and used binoculars at the top.

When he came down again, he had little to report. 'This copse is low lying. Can't see as far as you'd think. No signs of enemy activity, though, in any direction. Roads appear to be clear for the moment.'

Lofty dropped down in the circle of men, who were smoking and looking thoughtful.

'Tanks, or mobile infantry we have to look out for,' Johnson pointed out, in his best lecturing manner. 'I don't think Jerry has a base all that close. At least, not in this valley. Any land forces sent after us won't necessarily reach us before dark.'

'Think it's worthwhile hangin' on till dark, Corp?' Jock Pawson asked.

'They could pulverize us from the air, if we ventured out before!' Nick pointed out bluntly.

The sapper ducked his head, and patiently waited for Johnson to give his instructions. The Liverpudlian smoked with his hands on his hips. 'This road is out of our way, but we're committed to it for a while to let the Major get close to the tank harbour unseen.'

'We'll rest up here till the light's goin' then we'll push on towards the next line of foothills. There's a winding track going up. We'll give Jerry's armour a chase, if he comes after us, an' then watch our chance to break away an' join our mates. Is that understood?'

There were no queries. Sentries were posted, and the rest of the troop settled down to sleep. Their repose was untroubled, and some could have gone on sleeping when they were roused an hour before sunset to take a meal. They ate doggedly while they watched the changing colours on the high ground to westward.

Soon, they were making inroads into their meagre supplies of tobacco and awaiting the order to move out. The combination led the way at dusk. The others followed, and gradually the long flat stretch which separated them from the base of the winding hill track seen through the glasses dwindled away.

The mules played up as the combination pointed the way up the sloping track, but there were too many determined troopers about to put up with their tantrums for long. Johnson took the outfit round the first loop of track and there he found a kind of crude lay-by. The extra space was all the excuse he needed to call a halt until daybreak.

★ ★ ★

The mules were the first to awake after dawn. Their cries for food and attention finally roused the men and the lay-by became the scene of modest activity. While preparations were made for breakfast, Johnson and Burrows walked half way round the next loop. They were smoking cigarettes and swinging binoculars by their straps.

The N.C.O. chose to look down into the valley while the sapper studied the route ahead. Both saw interesting sights through their lenses, but Johnson's was the most urgent. Coming across from the copse where they had been dive-bombed were four tanks. As no Allied tanks were in the area, they were German, and almost certainly a part of the squadron seen earlier — the Tigers. Nick grabbed Johnson's glasses, not wanting to waste time in focusing his own. A mere five seconds were sufficient to confirm what the Corporal had seen. They raced back to their fellows, and spread the alarm.

'Out, out, out!' Johnson yelled. 'Tiger tanks comin' across the flats after us! Forget the breakfast! Take a swig of hot water if it's boiled an' let's get movin'. Everybody ready in five minutes, mules an' all!'

'Permission to ditch the combo, Corp!' Nick requested, grinning through his jet beard.

Scouse's bleached fair brows shot up his forehead. 'Whatever for? Won't it be a lot more use if we're goin' to be chased?'

'Might be more use still if it had a part in blasting some of the track away. There's a biggish drop down to the valley floor!'

'Mines?'

'A single mine under it, an' perhaps a booby trap for one of the bright boys, eh?'

Johnson shuddered and backed away. 'Okay, Burrows, I suppose you know best. But Pongo won't like you much now he's got used to that sidecar an' I don't feel like footsloggin' up this 'ill on an empty stomach!'

Thirteen men, plus two carts and the trolley were ready to move off on time. Pongo stayed behind to help Nick with his destructive efforts. Between them they scraped out a small hole deep enough to take a regulation-sized mine. The hole was about three yards from the outer edge of the track and in a position calculated to cause maximum subsidence. Nick refused to let Pongo fill it in. Neither would he allow him to touch the device which he fitted to the handlebars of the bike.

Pongo's nerves suffered as the iron-clads rumbled up the first of the gradient. He felt like saying he might just as well have gone ahead with the rest, but he knew such an attitude was unreasonable.

'Get started, if you want, Pongo,' Nick murmured.

He bent really close and examined his device from all angles. At last, he was satisfied. They set off together and rounded the first of the loops before their neck hairs stopped prickling.

★ ★ ★

As the first Tiger came round the bend and the combination was revealed, the head and shoulders of the commander appeared out of his turret. He focused his glasses on it, and remained suspicious. It could have been abandoned because of a mechanical failure. On the other hand, it could have been put there for some special purpose. He turned down an offer from one of his crew who wanted to inspect it from close-up.

'Driver, I want you to approach it very cautiously. Edge it as gently as you can over the precipice. Got that?'

The driver repeated his instructions. He manœuvred behind the machine and started to push it from the rear as the nose of his tank came round. The booby trap attached to the handlebars was in this way avoided, but as soon as a wheel rolled over the planted mine the explosive detonated and up went the combo.

Earth and small stones flew in all directions. A deep rumble carried to those in the iron-clad's innards. They saw the tangle of scrap, all that remained of the combination, go over the cliff along with upwards of a ton of soil. The subsidence edged nearer and nearer to the forward end of the tracks, but a prompt move on the part of the driver prevented a catastrophe. The tank was hurriedly and jerkily backed away from the imminent danger, and while it was manœuvred at an angle of thirty degrees from the horizontal past the tricky spot, the commander sent back a curt warning to those who followed.

After that, the chase was on. The tanks were manœuvred at high speed, and just over an hour had gone by when the leading iron-clad got a good sighting of the fleeing party rounding the outer side of a track loop higher up.

Toiling men were helping the mules haul the carts up the gradient. One cart seemed much slower than the other and it remained in view when the rest had rounded the bend and were out of sight. The commander barked orders to his crew.

The barrel of the gun swung up. The range was hastily worked out, and one shell flew across space in an effort to eliminate the toilers. It dropped within ten yards of the cart, and sent up a shower of earth which panicked the men and the animal. A wooden disc wheel snapped across the middle and suddenly the cart was slipping towards the abyss.

More soil crumbled away from the feet

of the men who fought to save the cart. They scrambled clear and the grabbed for the equipment in the back of the cart. The driver hurriedly slashed through the harness holding the animal. It kicked itself clear and went off round the next bend with the men in pursuit.

They did not need any coaxing as the whining of the next shell had started. Fortunately, they were able to round the bend before it blasted them to eternity. By this time, every paratrooper had half moons of perspiration under his arms and a wet patch between the shoulder blades. Running away from armour was no joke. They had to keep going, or go under. And they knew from intelligent hearsay that the German tank crews did not always bother to use a gun on running men.

Sometimes they just rolled them into the ground . . .

Scouse Johnson, himself, was the man who caught the racing mule and made it possible for it to be harnessed to the surviving cart, ahead of its mate. After that, the uphill running rate improved for a while. Nick was one of the last of the group to look for a short ride on the cart.

He actually asked permission, and Johnson frowned on him with a brow as black as thunder because he needed all his breath for forward progress. The Corporal gestured with a thumb for him to get aboard, a feat which Nick accomplished at the second scrambling attempt.

He used his binoculars to good effect, even though he had to keep wiping the salt sweat off the eye lenses. He had spotted something beyond the next loop which suggested a change of exertion. He shouted as much, but the others only nodded and were content to find out what fate had in store for them when they reached it.

At the next critical spot, a wheel was blasted off the trolley. Wright and Pawson promptly abandoned it and crawled into safety on their hands and knees. As they straightened up, a remarkable sight took their attention. At the innermost end of a loop of track, in a similar position to where their night's stop had been, they saw the beginnings of a village of sorts.

This was more than a cutback. It was a wide space with an area of more than an acre. Leading up to the flat expanse was a sloping corduroy ramp; that is to say, a soil slope with the boles of long slim trees beaten into it to anchor the soil in the rainy season.

About a dozen adobe dwellings were scattered about the secluded spot, but there were no humans in sight, and no lesser animals, for that matter. The paratroopers raced for the corduroy slope, knowing that they could not keep ahead on the winding track indefinitely.

Nick Burrows, however, slowed to a walk and gave the new area a more extensive scrutiny before going in close. On the heights behind the 'village' he saw other habitations which blended into the landscape with surpassing ease. There were conical shaped huts thatched with turf, or simply with the leaves of trees. Doubtless, their basic frame was a kind of wicker work.

The nearest of these unusual huts were perhaps four hundred yards above the adobes. Either they were inhabited by very agile people, or else there had to be some way of getting up to the higher level.

The men raced the cart, pulled by the two mules, over the logs. As the ground levelled out, they stopped and looked round for instructions. Johnson was blown, and all he could do was push them further back. Nick overtook him and laid a gentle hand on his shoulder.

'Will you act on what I say, Scouse?'

Johnson nodded. 'Have the men occupy the rearmost of the huts, and be prepared to pull out if you hear me shout. All right?'

As soon as his chest eased down, the Corporal gave his instructions. The cart was rushed to one side, out of sight. The men hurried to the rear of the site. Only Ginger Potts stayed with the N.C.O. and he was careful to crouch low. Within a few minutes their ears were entertained by the jolting and grinding noise of the first tank.

Johnson said: 'We've got to wait till it's at the bottom of that ramp an' then roll these! All right?'

'What 'appens if we don't stop 'em?' Ginger asked soberly.

Scouse watched him fingering his grenade as though it was a piece of fruit. 'We get out o' the line of fire an' make for the back! Don't forget that!' He was thinking about four second fuses, and wondering if the grenades had enough time to roll down the slope as far as the tank. If they stopped short, they'd blow the logs out of the slope, but perhaps that would not be a bad thing.

Potts squeezed his arm, and made him listen more carefully. A mule sounded off to one side of them, as though giving the alarm. Ginger stared at Johnson with his brows raised. The Corporal nodded. With great deliberation they raised their grenades right-handed to their mouths, gently pulled out the pins and rolled them towards the slope with all the deliberation of crown green bowlers.

Down went the explosives in a series of small bounces. One of them went off course and exploded ahead of the tank. The other actually hit the side but failed to blow off a track. Johnson rose to his feet and manhandled Potts after him. They ducked away to one side, ran to the outer limit of the plateau and turned for the rear.

'Stand by, lads!' Johnson gasped. 'We've got trouble any time now!'

Someone called them into an adobe. They dashed in and sank down, gasping. The tank's progress over the tree boles shook the whole area. A shell blasted into the bank between the rearmost adobes. A heavy machine-gun sprayed the dwellings nearer the ramp. Presently, the tank commander grew curious. The machine-gun accounted for the mules, which howled in agony as they died, and still no surprise attack was mounted against the armour.

The first iron-clad was slowly turned to the left. With great deliberation, the driver pushed in the end of the adobe on that side. It was empty, and its imminent demolition produced no reaction. The adobe in the other direction received the same treatment.

Meanwhile, the paratroopers looked to Johnson who was fresh out of ideas and hoping against hope that Burrows would come up with something. Another adobe was reduced to dust as the perspiring sapper appeared in the doorway of the hut which Johnson had entered.

'A way out, up the rear slope!' he panted. 'We'll have the drop on them with a vengeance when we get up there!'

Gasping as he was, Nick's voice sounded deadly. The others took heart from him. Potts was the first on his feet, and leading the way round the back. Nick pointed to the far corner, which looked to be thick with hanging foliage.

'Must get the rest of the boys over here without causing too much fuss, Scouse!'

Potts, and Lofty Wright, who had a low penetrating voice, undertook to pass the word along. Nick led Johnson, and the other seven men from the hut into the corner, and pointed to the bottom end of a corduroy staircase. This was steeper and much narrower than the ramp which led to the adobes, and the tree boles jutted out from the soil more like steps than a continuous surface. The men took courage from the sight. To some of them, at least, it was like a ladder leading to paradise. Johnson gave Nick the thumbs up sign, and cautiously began to lead the way. He was still blown at the start, and he had several hundred steps to negotiate. He hoped they wouldn't meet with hostiles at the top.

The rest of the paras waited until the tank was occupied again before scampering across to the stairway. Fortunately, they were not seen. Nick took them up at a slow economic pace which he thought would best suit the climb. The steps were steep enough for it to be inadvisable to look down, though several men were sorely tempted as the sounds of continued destruction carried up to them.

At last, they came out at the top. And there they saw the handful of natives who lived in the thatched huts. Seven of them were children. Five of these were walking about, and the youngest were at the breasts of two of the women. Two bearded men, short in stature and very stocky, came forward shyly to greet them. They appeared to be father and son.

Everyone in this small family unit was

dressed in thick woollen garments. Their feet were protected by sandals and broad cloths of the Bedouin type covered their heads. The late-comers were led into a clearing between the huts where a lamb's carcass was turning on a spit over a fire. Unfortunately, these people knew no French, and none of the soldiers could understand the Arab dialect. Some communication was possible, however, through sign language.

Johnson left Nick Burrows in charge of liaison while he went to the edge of the smaller high plateau with Ginger Potts and those two inseparables, Jock Pawson and Lofty Wright. They manœuvred themselves into a position where they could see the last of the adobes being pushed down by the leading tank.

Two others had moved into the arena, and the fourth one waited on the outer track at the bottom of the ramp. This, Johnson judged, was a critical time. He and his men watched without making any sound. Presently, Nick joined him. The first thing he was told heightened his interest.

'They haven't found the way we came up here, mate,' Ginger said.

'More than that,' Scouse went on. 'They're baffled. An' this far nobody's shown himself out of a turret. Think we should wait? They'll never get a tank up here, an' that lamb smells good!'

In shifting his position, Johnson unfortunately loosened a small patch of earth. It rolled down the steep slope into the dusty, rubble-strewn place below. One of the tanks spotted it. It was difficult to aim a gun barrel at that high angle, but a heavy machine-gun elevated easily enough.

A burst of bullets sent the watchers further back, and holes were torn in the sides of two huts. No attempt was made to retaliate. Nick counselled patience. He and the Corporal had their food brought to them. An hour later, they were still gnawing when a turret flap came open and the crew of the first tank cautiously emerged.

This was what the paras were waiting for. Three grenades all failed to go into the turret, but they burst close around it.

Germans cowered in all directions, but thanks to their sterling efforts against the adobes there was nowhere they could hide. Aimed down at that angle, the Brens were lethal. One after another, the men of the tank crew were cut down. Soon they were all eliminated. When a second tank manœuvred to get its gun trained up the slope, a few wildly thrown grenades dissuaded its crew.

The third tank turned about and made a run to get out of the danger zone. In lumbering down the ramp, it blocked the aim of the fourth tank, which was the only one capable of hitting the higher village with shells.

As the iron-clads retreated to the lower ground with their mission unfulfilled, the small handful of men who had thwarted them were already thinking about an alternative route to get them towards the south-east.

7

The nearer the main party of paratroops got to the tank harbour and the time planned for their attack, the greater was the strain on brains and nerves. The timing made steady progress essential, and yet secrecy was every bit as important. There were times between halts when the target appeared to be keeping its distance, and some of the more disillusioned paras dreamed that the iron-clad workshop was a mirage.

Dunstable felt the strain more than anyone. During the last day or two he had temporarily forgotten his compulsive desire to win for himself rapid promotion. More so than ever before, he identified himself with the men under his command.

A good deal of the night after quitting the farm was spent in a steady march towards the map location. Progress was slow, but steady, and as his footsteps flagged, he reconciled himself by recollecting that this last night march gave them an even chance of locating the harbour at the time planned all those days before back in Algiers, and since confirmed to Corporal Johnson.

A mere hour before dawn, Captain Burns, his second in command, stumbled over a series of small rocks which brought him up short. Using his masked torch, the Captain discovered that he was standing on the rim of a circular depression about a hundred yards across. He called the C.O.'s attention to this, and the column was halted.

Accompanied by two troopers, the Captain investigated the depression more closely, and soon he was back and enthusing over the find.

'No signs of human habitation at all, sir. Soft sand and a few rocks and boulders to break up the view from the sky. Dawn near enough on us. I suggest we move the whole outfit in there, prepare a meal and settle down for a few hours' rest. We can put out a few keen men to recce ahead and see how far the target is.'

Dunstable waved him into silence. He

had heard enough. Quiet orders were passed down the line, and the human crocodile moved thankfully into cover. Fires were lit with some caution. They served to take the chill out of the North African dawn, and also to cook food.

Small scouting parties moved out after a short rest. About midday, two groups of three came back feeling tired, hot and dry, but far from dispirited. Their joint revelations established beyond all doubt the location of the tank harbour.

All officers were called together to hear the reports. The harbour and workshop were less than three miles away, in a depression similar to the one in which the outfit was sheltering, except that the one used by the Germans was much bigger. The bedrock round the sides of it was broken up in places, and there the gates were placed in the encompassing wire fence.

Guards in greatcoats were patrolling the inside of the wire fence at intervals. The most unusual feature of the place was a camouflaging flat 'roof' of chain-linked metal, such as is sometimes used for hurriedly constructed airstrips in desert and jungle. Painted tarpaulins were draped across the mesh to kill the glint of metal and to camouflage it from the sky.

Although the scouts had not been able to get nearer than three hundred yards, they were able to describe the harbour with confidence as being extensive. The infrequent comings and goings of cars, jeeps and tanks seemed to suggest that possibly a hundred or two of German personnel were on the strength of the place, not counting tanks crews who might be waiting and resting. Every officer was given the chance to question the scouts. More information came to light.

Burns, who had worked his body into the soft sand, puffed contentedly at his pipe. The camouflage net over everything had intrigued him and set his imagination to work. He withdrew his pipe and held it up.

'Gents, this net might help us a lot. If, as we've been told, it is covered with painted tarps, then clearly the people underneath it can't see through. They'll have small anti-aircraft gun nests, but they won't be under the net, they'll be wide of it.

'It seems to me that we could create a diversion by lobbing a few explosives on the net! Then, while Jerry is reacting, we could blast in the gates and make our strike!'

A murmur of approval came from the listeners. They enthused over Burns' idea, which was to have an important part in the strike.

★   ★   ★

Within an hour of the German tanks withdrawing, Corporal Johnson's troop had left the remote hill village. The younger of the two Arabs showed them animal paths which quickly took them down to the valley floor. At the lower level, they rested, and when they had patiently made it clear to the guide which direction they intended to take, he stayed with them for another hour. In that time, he discovered one more useful path which helped them over another ridge and into the next valley down which the tank harbour was supposed to be located.

Every man in the party wrung the Arab's hand. They gave him cigarettes and little titbits from their packs, and went on their way assured that he would not put the Boche onto them. Weariness made them take an hour's rest in the afternoon. It was an hour which dragged to an hour and a half. Any other time, Johnson would not have insisted on a move, but he knew that zero hour for the strike against the tank harbour was at dusk, and they felt honour bound to be up with their comrades at the time of the trial of strength.

They were still walking in the right direction but short of their objective when the light began to fade. Every fifteen minutes after dusk they took it in turns to be hoisted up on shoulders to study the terrain ahead through the binoculars.

Exactly one hour after dark, Jock Pawson's short powerful limbs were draped round the neck of his buddy, Lofty Wright. Jock panned the glasses through almost half a circle. He hung on for some reason, and just as Lofty was thinking of putting him on the ground, the first explosion occurred up ahead.

It was far enough off to be muted, but every man guessed correctly that the other paras were in action. Grim laughter signified approval, even though they were not there to take part. Corporal Johnson and Nick Burrows were hastily hoisted aloft for a further survey of the scene of the action.

Johnson was pestered for information. 'It has to be the tank harbour! Explosives are bursting over it right now! Not from the sky, I think! They all seem to be on the same level!'

'Probably a protective ceiling of some sort,' Nick put in.

'There goes the alarm buzzer,' Pawson added.

Again, the sound was muted by distance, but there was no difficulty in identifying it. All three observers reported another explosion, this time at a lower level. They assumed that a gate had been blasted in. After that, the night silence was constantly broken by tracer, grenades and other explosives of every description.

One after another, the three men with

the glasses were lowered into the midst of their friends. 'What now, Corp?' Potts queried.

Johnson rasped his beard, and put his fingers through the thinning hair on his crown. 'Well, we're all pretty tired and we haven't made it in time, but there might still be something we can do if we keep going. I'd say we have a couple of miles to walk. What do you think, Nick?'

'Two to three miles,' the sapper confirmed. 'I'm not sure it would be a good thing to press on right up to the scene of the action, though. After all, we don't know when our party will be comin' away, an' when they do they won't want anything to delay them. We might be a liability after all the punishing miles we've done today.'

Nick's statement was not popular, but most of the men agreed with him. Johnson knew this by their silence. 'All right, then,' he said, at last, 'we'll go a bit nearer and we don't rush it. If there's any signs of our blokes comin' away, we'll change our direction an' make for Allied lines. That seems to be about all! Let's go!'

They moved off in threes. Five minutes

later, a noise in a different direction made it necessary to use the glasses again. This time Potts was the lookout, and he was looking towards the rear.

'Bad news, lads,' he murmured. 'Jerries overtakin' us. Motorized. Masked 'eadlights. One big lorry an' two 'alf tracks! They'll be along in five to ten minutes. Reinforcements for the tank repairers!'

'We've got to stop them,' Johnson muttered. 'Point is, though, how? Do we just dig in here an' blast 'em as they go by, or try somethin' more spectacular?'

'If we could put them on the wrong track, Scouse, an' shoot them up into the bargain,' Nick ventured.

This time a few weary troopers were not inclined to listen. Potts rather unexpectedly backed Burrows' idea. 'Why don't we trot forward for an 'undred yards or so? See if we can find a good spot to dig in, or better still a place to divert the drivers!'

Ginger nudged Burrows and the pair set off at a stumbling trot. Johnson capitulated at once, and the rest followed, not wanting to be separated with lorry loads of Germans at their backs. They strained their eyes to see ahead, and presently a derelict lorry with Italian markings presented itself at a turn in the track.

The party pulled up, panting for breath. 'Don't swarm all over it,' Nick warned, 'it may be booby-trapped.'

He switched on his torch and gave it a quick scrutiny. It had been shot up, presumably by a plane. Although it was a Lancia it had been used by Germans, as certain items in the back showed. He clambered up into the rear and called to the others.

'Any chance of another track anywhere abouts?' he enquired.

'No ruddy chance at all,' Potts answered. He was getting jumpy, and the wheels of the pursuing vehicles were affecting everyone else.

For a time, the healthy explosions at the tank harbour were ignored. Dunstable's determined outfit had blasted its way in. They were using their weapons and explosives in one glorious sortie of fighting and demolition. They offered no quarter, and expected none.

'Ginger's wrong, you know!'

Lofty Wright was the man who had contradicted. He had wandered a few yards away. His voice attracted half a dozen others, anxious to see why Potts was wrong. They stumbled over to him and found themselves at the beginning of a lesser track which diverged from the one leading to the harbour.

'Just what we've been looking for!' Johnson yelled. 'What now, Burrows?'

'I want you to push over this truck, but wait till I get out first. It has to block the proper route. I'm going to try and sell the drivers the idea the usual road has been mined! Are you with me?'

Nick scrambled down with a brush and a tin of white paint. It had been used before, and some of the paint had dried down the outside. He reached into the back and pulled out an old wooden door, which he moved on one side with his other items. Every man's shoulder went under the truck, and within two minutes it was on its side, effectively blocking the normal route.

Nick propped his door at the back of it

where it would be seen instantly by trucks coming from the north.

He said: 'Scouse? I should take the boys about a hundred yards down that other track. Give 'em a good old pasting with the Brens an' such like when they come along. Then retreat. Try an' draw them after you.'

In spite of the close proximity of trouble, Johnson grinned as he watched Nick's brushwork. First, the sapper produced a reasonable facsimile of a death's head skull. Then, underneath it, he scrawled the words *Achtung! Minen!* Finally, he drew an arrow, pointing away in the new direction.

'Yer, that's the idea, mate,' Johnson answered. 'But you can come along with us now. You've finished your art lesson.'

'I'll stay, if you don't mind, Scouse. Just in case they aren't taken in with my handiwork. If all goes well, I'll be walking off in a direction a few degrees south of west. You do the same. Cross the proper route and keep on going. I'll try and contact you around midnight. I'm afraid we're likely to want every scrap of energy we've got left, after this little caper.'

Johnson shook him by the hand and scampered off to lead the rest away to the ambush. The sounds of the approaching German troops gave Nick butterflies in his stomach.

There had been a time when he thought he didn't need his fellow men all that much. It had been shortly after the shock death of his father and stepmother. When he volunteered for the paras, he had been ducking out, in a way. But now, as he waited, very much alone in the middle of an alien country, at night, he felt that the events which had occurred since his last jump had changed him.

He did not feel quite so bitter towards others. And loneliness accentuated the sure knowledge that he belonged with the small party of men who had just trotted off to implement the ambush. What a pity they were not all airborne sappers like himself. Even if they survived, and got back to the Allied lines, he and the others were almost certain to be separated. With a sudden flash of insight, he knew that his growing confidence in his fellow men might go back on him, if that happened.

He struggled to quell the queasiness in his stomach and succeeded to some extent. The bobbing headlights of the leading vehicle were only a hundred yards away, and but for the fact that they were masked to hide the beam, he must have been seen.

He crouched low behind the truck and gradually worked his way further down the road. Some twenty yards away, he came across a big boulder which stood three feet above the soil. He decided that he ought to use it for shelter. After squeezing himself in behind it, and making sure his weapons were to hand, he thought about the possibilities.

One thing which he had overlooked gave him a touch of nerves. The wet paint on the board! What if the drivers saw that it was fresh and became suspicious? He tried to shrug away the consideration, and was only partially successful.

Two minutes later, the lorry stopped. The driver, and an officer in the cab, shouted to one another. A powerful torch shone on the board and a brief discussion took place. The torch was trained down the track behind the derelict Lancia. It hovered over the boulder which concealed Nick, and then passed on.

Presently, the officer started shouting all over again. The distant explosions at the tank harbour prompted his impatience. A feldwebel jumped to the ground and went looking for the alternative route. He found it almost at once and shouted back to the cab.

He was ordered back on board. Within seconds the lorry was being turned in the new direction. The ruse had worked, but how much more effective a few real mines would have been instead. Unfortunately, when the troops' deficiencies were made good, mines seemed to have been overlooked. Nick had never been quite sure whether the main party was in short supply or not.

Off went the lorry behind its bobbing shortened headlight beams. The first half-track vehicle followed it without question. So did the second. And then the area round about the derelict truck started to get quiet. It was time to go.

Nick consulted his watch and his wrist compass. He collected his few essential belongings and stepped out along his pre-arranged course. A few minutes later, the staccato crackle of Stens and Brens filled the air. The three vehicles stopped hurriedly, and their packed occupants started to drop to the ground on the quiet side.

Skilfully thrown grenades landed in the half-tracks and several troopers did not live to reach the ground. For two or three minutes, the bursts continued without ceasing. Just when the volume of enemy fire was beginning to swell, Johnson's outfit packed up and the Krauts had no flashes to fire at.

Nick increased his pace. Loneliness gave him energy when he thought his stamina had gone back on him. He stumbled across his friends fifteen minutes before midnight and was absorbed into their midst. About the time when the Focke-Wulfs started to approach from the north, Jock Pawson stumbled into a dry ditch some three feet in depth.

The air was filled with pithy sayings in pure Glaswegian. Lofty bent down to help him out, but the sudden lighting up of the sky by a flare made him jump down instead. As one man, the others followed him. Another flare followed, and directly under the second one scores of paras were streaming away from the tank harbour in full view of anyone who cared to look.

They started to cower lower in the bright light, and in response to a curt order, they split up into smaller groups but kept moving. One man turned a Bren on a plane, but did it little harm.

Johnson was restless in the bottom of the ditch. He was wondering if there was anything at all they could be doing to improve the lot of their fellows.

'Stop worrying, Scouse,' Nick muttered. 'There are times when we can't help at all. This is one of them. We all feel as badly about it as you do. Your job now is to get us back to Allied lines. Tomorrow morning will be early enough for a start, too.'

Soon, an artillery battery, directed to the target by the planes which had dropped the flares, started to bracket the area of the paras' retreat. Some sank into places of concealment, but others, realistically thinking about their situation on the morrow, kept steadily moving towards the west.

In time, the guns became more accurate. Group after group of the scurrying marauders were caught in the blasts of explosions. The men in the ditch felt every shell explode. It was almost as if they were taking a personal physical beating. There were cries, some scarcely human, which made it hard for the listeners in hiding to rest.

The artillery, and subsequent flares made it possible for the lorried infantry to overtake the retreating paras. The running action dragged on until within an hour of dawn. By that time, Corporal Johnson's weary team were all sleeping the sleep of exhaustion. They knew nothing until the sun started to warm the earth, and even then they were reluctant to crawl out into the open and find out the worst.

8

For three days after that glorious strike against the tank harbour Johnson's little troop stayed within two miles of the place. A furlong away from the dry drain into which Jock Pawson had stumbled, they found for themselves a hideout in a big roofless barn of a place with huge pebbled walls.

The building was in the middle of a large plot of land which had once been cultivated. Some time previous to the war, however, a germ in the soil had persuaded its Arab owner that his future lay elsewhere. The pebble barn was the only building still standing to mark his former holdings.

The fifteen men were extremely lucky to get into the barn without being apprehended by the small patrols of prowling German troopers.

They did so, and kept well out of sight while members of the main party of paratroopers were being apprehended over an area of five square miles. Nobody in the party was in any hurry to do anything.

Their bodies were tired. They needed sustaining meals with plenty of vitamins and a long long rest in a place where the nerves could be relaxed. Their bruises, cuts and abrasions were slow to heal. One or two began to suffer with indigestion, and others had a touch of dysentry which left them feeling unlike exercise of any kind.

For some reason, their roofless and windowless abode was missed out of the thorough inspection carried out by enemy ground troops.

Gradually, the aches went out of their bodies, but they were slow to pick up on energy. All they were able to do in those seventy-two hours, apart from resting and eating was to dig two long slits in the soil floor of the barn. One they used as a daytime toilet, and the other was utilized so that they could walk up and down indoors for exercise without fear of their heads and shoulders being seen through the doorway or the windows.

Three things prompted them to move on after three days. One was the knowledge that the prowling German infantry was withdrawing from the area. The second was the rate at which they were running through their essential food supplies. The third, and perhaps the most telling of all, was a deterioration in the weather. Heavy rainclouds began to scud across the sky, and not infrequently drenching showers came through their non-existence roof and drove them under their capes, or into their jumping smocks.

Potts, a known moaner, was on his best form when the rains came, but he did not have things all his own way. About half a dozen of the others began to use their tongues to excess, and as a result the limiting space in the barn appeared to shrink. They were too closely thrust in upon one another for men in their state.

They had no clear idea of how far they would have to walk to find the nearest Allied lines. All they knew was that they would be hard pushed to make it, even with luck on their side. Late in the afternoon of the third day, Scouse called his men to order.

'Now look here, you blokes. It's our bounden duty to make our way back to the British lines. Nobody's goin' to ask where we've been loiterin' since we did our jobs, but we can't stay here for ever. Some of us are plannin' to move on tonight. I ought to order you to march off together, but I'm not going to. If you want to break up into smaller groups, it's all right by me. Now's the time to state your views on the matter. What do you say?'

Two of the moaners sounded off. They were both very much in favour of staying in one bunch, although they could not offer any telling reasons for their views. It was Jock Pawson, who cleared his throat rather noisily and expressed the view of the average man.

'In other circumstances, we might have done well for ourselves in smaller groups. But the natives aren't well off, anyway. An' we're short on stamina an' in no great shape to defend ourselves if the occasion arises. For that reason alone, we ought to stick together, an' if necessary, we'll go down fighting together.'

At the end of his short speech, the Scotsman's voice was drowned in a brief vocal uproar, which Johnson was quick to quieten.

'I take it I've heard the views of you all now. That being so, it only remains to tell you you'll be fell in for departure a half hour after sunset. So how about quietening down now so we can get some rest? We might have to travel miles before we find another spot like this.'

Some dozed, and others passed round cigarettes. When the weapons came out for oiling and cleaning a small though subtle change came over the party. They were unconsciously girding themselves for the supreme effort required to get them back among friends.

★   ★   ★

Although the feet of many of them were covered in blisters, the majority agreed to Nick Burrows' suggestion to march a little further south than the obvious route back to Allied lines. His hunches in the past had not let them down, and the fact that he was an ordinary bloke using his brains no longer bothered anyone. His distrust of the average Arab led many of the men to become petty thieves. When they did not want to make contact with the natives they watched their chance to steal a few eggs or vegetables, and on one or two occasions they grabbed chickens and stuffed them into their emptying packs.

No one could really call it looting on the scale which they worked.

During the first night on the move, the weather appeared to be acting against them. So severe was the downpour that everywhere the earth's surface was turned to mud. Their feet slithered on ground which they had never seen before, and the slow forward progress was something of a nightmare. Every man among them longed to be back in the roofless barn with the raindrops pattering off his smock.

Eventually, a bleak sun brought the steam out on their clothing in a copse above an adobe hamlet.

On the second day, a hedge-hopping plane took them unawares and sent streams of tracer perilously close to trembling bodies, but they succeeded in avoiding troops who came looking for them later in a small half-track lorry.

Forty-eight hours went by. A woman whose face was draped with a yashmak started to follow them. They were too tired to wonder how pretty her face was behind the cloth, and most of them wanted her to simply walk away. But she persisted, and when Nick finally tried to find out what she was after, she insisted on their following her.

This put them very much on the alert. Nick, Ginger and Scouse moved ahead behind the woman with their Stens held ready. The other twelve formed three sides of a square and came along twenty yards behind, prepared for the worst. She led them directly towards a dried out watercourse. At the very rim of it, she stopped between two tufts of grass and looked back. Her eyes appeared to be smiling. Shrugging slightly, she stepped down into the hollow and kept on walking.

The advance trio paused on the brink. Potts' keen ears heard a distant whisper. Some of the tension went out of his face, and he indicated with a gesture that he would be glad to go first. Johnson gave ground, but followed close behind, flanked by Nick.

All three spotted a man on his knees some twenty yards away. He was a sergeant who had been with the main party. Instead of diving for a cave-like opening in the damp sand, he half raised his hands. His mouth dropped open. A Sten barrel stuck out from a grassy hummock quite close to him.

Ginger said: 'If you 'orrible Red Devils are not decently dressed for visitors we'll back out an' call another day!'

A hidden man shouted, and within a minute upwards of a score of troopers wormed their way out of the sand and rushed to meet the new party. Standing to the rear of them were the padre, whose head was bandaged, and Major Dunstable with his left arm in a sling. The C.O. had long since run out of tobacco, but his pipe was comfortably clenched between his teeth.

Somehow, the extra fifteen men fitted themselves into the crowded dugouts in the wadi. Food was put into a common pool and shared out afresh. A torrential downpour occurred, and rain slopped under the doors, but nothing stopped the lively exchange of conversation until after the sun was well down in the west.

That night, the airstrip strike force turned in with the padre's spoken prayers. It made a change, and helped to offset the griping private worries about all the scores of men who had given their lives in the elimination of the tanks, their crews and the maintenance unit.

The next day they moved on again after restoring the whole of the string of wadi dugouts to the Arab woman and her self-effacing family. One of her sons reconnoitred the way ahead for them, and mentioned a friendly farmer who might give them assistance.

From that time forward, the survivors met with no more treachery.

Exactly twenty-one days after they had dropped from the skies, they were walking in single file down a new watercourse brought on by the persistent winter rains. The water was six to nine inches deep, and the stream bed was on low ground, of course. This meant that it could not be seen from any great distance, and gave the trudging men enough confidence to keep going. Visibility was reduced to a few yards by the driving rain, and the harsh command, when it came, was almost drowned out by the pattering of water.

For no special reaon, Johnson and Company were leading the way.

The Corporal squinted past dripping raindrops and saw a stocky officer in a pillbox hat standing a few yards up the slope with his feet apart. A rifle protruded towards them from under his gas cape, and to one side three crouching soldiers sat behind a machine-gun on a tripod stand. The weapon was partially covered by a light tarpaulin. Other armed figures stood about scarcely in visibility.

Johnson remained standing where he was, but made no attempt to drop his weapon. Nick came up with him, and squinted over his shoulder. The sapper felt fairly sure that they were confronted by Frenchmen.

He raised a hand, rather jerkily and continued to go forward into shouting distance. The effect of this move was nearly disastrous. The officer almost fired his weapon, and the machine-gunner drew a bead on his chest.

Nick came to a halt. He called: '*Monsieur*, do not shoot! *Nous sommes Anglais!*'

He would have liked to have poured forth streams of fluent French, but his brain seemed drained with the rigours of the past few days, and he dried up. As it was, the French officer's suspicions grew. He barked short sharp instructions to his men without taking his eyes off the strangers or relaxing his vigilance. The word '*Boche*' was bandied back and forth. The French were of the opinion that Nick was a German pulling a smooth trick on them.

Just when it seemed that someone would be shot, the padre came forward, and in his best Sunday sermon voice, explained in fluent Parisian French just exactly who they were and how they came to be in that position. He offered no apology for Nick's atrocious accent, and at last the fierce expressions of the Foreign Legionnaires relaxed into smiles.

A remnant of the Red Devils had lived to fight another day.

Within a few hours they were moving across into Algeria in lorries.

9

It was on the 18th December that the remnants of the parachutists' strike force reached the Zimzim Rest Camp a few miles up the coast from Algiers. Four Arab villas formed the basic lodgings for the tired fighting men and housed the stores and the staff of cooks who were ordered to look after them.

Those who required medical treatment of any kind were, of course, weeded out on the first day. The rest merely pitched into the rooms of the villas, selected a bed and started to sleep off the long-term exhaustion brought on by the continued fighting and running of the past three weeks.

The temperature on the Algerian coast compared very favourably with the cold atmosphere of Tunisia with its mountains, its hills, its meandering valleys and its salt lakes. The paras were slowly kitted up again and made to feel respectable. When the sun was at its brightest, they were able to use the beach of white pebbles and warm sand.

Small tents sprang up all over the place as the men began to improve in health and outlook and showed an interest in the things around them. They ate, smoked, dozed, bathed and wrote letters home and wondered how many more hostile drops they would have to make before Montgomery had chased Rommel into Tunisia, and the combined 1st and 8th Armies had finally pushed the Afrika Korps out of Africa.

On the day before Christmas Eve, Nick, Scouse, Ginger and the others, none of whom had been separated so far, began to take an interest in the coming time of festivities. They took a ride on a jeep into Algiers and did some shopping in the Kasbah, collecting all they could in the way of fruit, vegetables and titbits of one sort and another. An enterprising Arab found a man who would sell them two or three chickens, but the price was high and the birds lacked some of the fleshiness they would have liked for such a special occasion as this.

The paras were up early on the morning of Christmas Day. Mail had been delayed, a thing which often happened with the forces overseas. Ginger gave it as his opinion that it had gone to the 8th Army by mistake, and seeing that the Desert Rats had only just entered Tripolitania behind the Afrikakorps, they stood to get it by about Easter of the following year.

Major Dunstable appeared for the meal at midday, although his arm was still in a sling, and he was thus handicapped for eating. However, he was in a cheerful mood and quick to see that his men were recovering their great zest for living. Beer was provided for every man who wanted it, and the C.O. paid for bottles of *Muscatel* out of his own pocket.

They drank to absent friends, but nobody asked about the actual figures for casualties. Everyone knew that a great many had failed to return, and they were content to leave it at that, knowing it was the grim fortune of war.

Unlike many men who had been in

Africa or the Mediterranean for a long time, the paras' faces were tender. It had required a very careful shave to take off the beards which they had grown subsequent to their last jump. For a time, they tended to shave only every other day until their skin again became accustomed to the regular bite of a razor.

By the time the Christmas meal was over, the dining hall was full of the smoke of cigarettes, tobacco and cigars. Men became bleary-eyed because of the atmosphere. The officers suggested that they should go out into the courtyard and take their drinks with them.

Apart from a few who were drunk, the other ranks agreed to this. A mouth organ was produced, and then a small concertina. The troops cheered themselves by singing songs about the war. Marching songs, and nostalgic ballads about the last 'all clear' and how they were going to resume where they left off when it was all over.

The postman sprang a special surprise by bringing in a late sorting of letters. This produced a wild and noisy round of applause, but tended to take some of the jollity out of the proceedings. Perhaps a score of men withdrew to their rooms to read mail from their sweethearts and wives. Others began to drink more heavily because they had received nothing.

The mouth organist ran out of breath and gradually the proceedings came to a quieter close. Nick, Ginger and Scouse all had a letter apiece. Perhaps Nick, the orphan, was the most surprised to receive one. He had no steady girl friend. To his surprise, it came from his sister-in-law, Lisa. She informed him that he was an uncle as she had given birth to a small dark girl by the name of Jeanne. Harry, she explained, was away. She hoped Nick had a pleasant Christmas, and that he might meet up with Harry some time soon.

Nick started to think about Harry all over again. The Reconnaissance Corps was a highly mobile outfit principally used for forward reconnoitring ahead of an army's front line. They were prepared to fight and to strike hard for vital information which would affect future plans. The way world events were shaping,

Harry was only likely to be in one of two places. Either just entering Tripolitania with the Eighth Army, or somewhere in that maze of mountains, hills and valleys which called itself Tunisia.

Somehow or another, Nick still thought it was likely to be the Eighth Army. He had a feeling that if new units of the Corps had arrived at Algiers for Tunisia he would have heard about it. This led him to think that he and his mates had learned very little about the conduct of the war through being in and around Algiers.

He was shrewd enough to think that there would be some changes directly the festive season was over. And he was about right.

Soon, his rather gloomy thoughts were interrupted by cross talk from Johnson and Potts. The Liverpudlian was engaged to a girl from the same city with long legs, a shape to dream about and a salty tongue which kept the wolves at bay. Potts, on the other hand, had hastily married his sweetheart, Mollie, so that she could be collecting a marriage allowance while he was away and thus building up a nice little bank account for when he finally got home.

For once, Potts was not moaning. 'Scouse, I can't think what you were thinking about not to get married the last time you were home! Think of all the money you're lettin' the Army keep when you could be drawin' a marriage allowance! You're positively chuckin' money away, mate! It ain't like you!'

Johnson raised himself on an elbow, looked across Pongo Smith's sleeping form, and asked: 'What's your missus doin' with 'erself, anyway?'

Ginger blinked. 'What's she doin'? Why, she's lookin' after 'er mother an' a younger brother an' sister, that's all! What should she be doing? She's lookin' after 'erself for me, that's what. An' by the hell she'd better be in good trim when I get home, too!'

Ginger coloured up when he saw Nick's eyes on him, but was still puzzled about Scouse's question.

'What made you ask me a question like that, Scouse?'

'Oh, I just wondered, wack. You see, my

bit of stuff, Pat, she's just got herself called up in the Wrens! She goes along to Portsmouth in about three days time. It'll make a change for 'er, I suppose, although you see a lot of matelots an' what not in Liverpool. I wonder 'ow she'll look in Navy uniform?'

Ginger thought about some cartoons he had seen in a men's magazine depicting ladies in and out of uniform. He was about to comment on them when he saw the seriousness of Johnson's face and a warning look on Nick's. Actually, Corporal Johnson was remembering what a fine looking girl Pat was. He was also remembering whispers of indiscretions committed by her older sister when she joined the A.T.S. In the back of his mind was a sneaking fear that she might meet some fellow in Royal Navy uniform who was a bit better educated and had more hair on the top of his head. This, however, was the sort of fear a fighting man did not communicate to his friends.

He yawned and pretended to be bored with the talk. Outside, a rain shower started to hit the cobbles and the nearby beach. Gradually, the sound it made lulled them to sleep.

★ ★ ★

Three days later, Major Dunstable began to interview his men rather formally. He talked about what was known of their performance in Tunisia, said what he could to encourage those who had little initiative, and told them that they would be wanted for some active training in a few days time.

Corporal Johnson came out with a bright light in his usually sombre, restless eyes. He had been recommended for his third stripe, and the chances were he would be wearing it before the month was out. He moved into a quiet corner where he screwed up his face to encourage telling phrases for a letter to Pat. Perhaps if he told her he was on top line for sergeant she wouldn't be in a hurry to toss him overboard for a Navy bloke.

Lofty Wright and Jock Pawson also came out looking very surprised. They went off together into a corner to discuss

162

jointly what the C.O. had said. Meanwhile, Nick Burrows, his mind occupied by a few unwelcome misgivings, moved into the room which Dunstable was using as an office.

He saluted, and when offered the chance, sat down in an upright chair on the opposite side of the desk from the Major.

'Well now, Burrows, according to everything I can find out, you've had quite a good campaign so far. We don't know what Lieutenant Casson thought about you, but everyone else who's been in touch since the Lieutenant's death seems to think very highly of you. Don't bother to blush, it makes good reading.

'I like the way you planned the demolition of those Stukas, and the way your intervention turned the tables on those Germans who had the drop on the rest of the section. You did a great job there, and on several occasions since. You have shown all the initiative of a capable leader. One thing bothers me. This far, you've shown no signs of wanting to take responsibility. Now why is that? Isn't it true you have a brother who is a commissioned officer?'

Nick flushed and bridled at the direct question. 'Well, yes sir, it's true my brother Harry is a captain, but then he has a flare for organizing people. It doesn't follow that I should be any good if I was placed in a position of authority. In any case, when I'm on active service, if I think of a worthwhile idea I shall always pass it on. I thought that having said this you might be satisfied with me.'

He ended rather lamely, and Dunstable grinned at him. 'I'm glad you spoke out, but I have to tell you that there will be countless occasions when the ordinary soldier will resent a man with no stripes on his arm giving his officers and N.C.O.s advice, however good it is.

'The men with the determination and the ideas ought to lead, and that's what I'm saying to you. Your ideas ought to be aired, always, and if you'd take more responsibility you'd certainly get the chance. I'd like you to think it over very seriously.'

Nick flashed his crooked grin. 'You may think this strange, sir, but I'm more concerned to keep in touch with the men I fought with in the last action than in taking promotion. I think comradeship in arms is very important. The men I came out with don't resent me. The trouble is that I'm a trained sapper and they are regular infantry.'

Dunstable was a long time in playing his trump card. 'Burrows, it may not be necessary for you to part from your former comrades. We are doing a certain amount of regrouping before we go into action again, plus some training for new arrivals. Now, if it happened that you were in the same troop as your fighting friends, although in a different section, that might change things. Having them around might give you confidence, I think. Bear this in mind when I ask you what you've decided. That'll be all for now, Burrows. Send the next man in.'

Back in the quarters in the villa, all the men were discussing the Major's interviews. Pawson and Wright had both been offered a corporal's stripes. Johnson told about his extra one, and Nick admitted that he had been sounded out for tapes.

To cut out a lot of ribald conjecture, which could be embarrassing, he snatched up his towel and trunks and made a dash for the beach.

Others followed. After the bathe, they talked more seriously. Johnson had more information than most. He reckoned that a new squadron was being formed quite soon; a squadron with only two troops, A and B. Captain Burns and another officer were to be the troop leaders. Several new section leaders were being drafted in.

The one they were specially interested in was Troop B, under Burns. The first section was to be sappers only, and the other three infantry. Some thirty new men would be arriving, who would be split evenly over the two troops.

The talk spread to the news of the war in Tunisia. British and American forces were engaged all along the mountainous spine of the country. As long as the Germans and their Italian Allies held control of the key mountains and passes which ringed Tunis and Bizerta, the country would continue to hold out against the British and Americans, and the ports would remain useful to Rommel, as well as to the troops garrisoning Tunisia.

In his spare time, Nick studied maps. Tunisia had a northern and an eastern seaboard. The mountains formed a mighty central bastion. And to the south there were a series of salt lakes which were impassable in winter. The kind of winter the British troops were experiencing in the mountains and hills seemed foreign to Africa, compared with the desert climate further east such as the Desert Rats had to cope with.

There was only one way of getting in behind the German defences in Tunisia, and that was to penetrate that small gap between the salt lakes and Gabes on the coast. It was known as the Gabes gap. Every day, Field Marshal Rommel backed his retreating Afrika Korps nearer to that gap, as he steadfastly kept ahead of the Eighth Army in the retreat through Tripolitania.

Nick wondered how it would all pan out.

★　★　★

The day before those men recommended for promotion were due to see the C.O. again, a staff officer wearing a captain's pips drove out from Algiers to the Rest Camp. He looked about him with obvious interest, and eventually wandered out on the beach in a pair of borrowed swimming trunks. He was a little over medium height, shaggy chested and long in the trunk like many accomplished sea swimmers.

He found Nick with surprising ease. Nick stood up and they shook hands. 'I'm Captain Jonathan Farne, schoolmaster turned soldier for the duration. I've got news for you, Burrows. I went through college with your brother. He left Algiers a week or so ago, and he asked me to look you up. Says he'll look forward to seeing you up Medjez way one of these days, and he hopes you'll be wearing something on your arm. He wants to remind you that you're of age now, and that hill fighting ought to suit you admirably, after the Lake District.'

Nick quickly overcame his embarrassment and chatted easily with the captain for a half hour or so. By the time the jeep went back into Algiers the sapper had almost made up his mind to accept promotion.

He did, in fact, do this and he entered into the spirit of the training of new arrivals with great gusto. The only thing he did not like about the new set-up was the slightly overbearing attitude of his section officer, one Lieutenant Harvey Maine, a Canadian who had left off controlling forest fires in his own country to come across and volunteer.

One day they mined a road. Another day they were required to discover where mines were laid. Then there was parachuting up the banks of the Wadi Zimzim. And lots of unarmed combat and map reading.

The day came when over the radio it was learned that Marshal Rommel's forces were now wholly in Tunisia; which meant that he was blocking the Gabes gap. Surely, the paratroopers thought, their next whirlwind drop into war could not be far off.

10

At last the day came. The orders were posted for the paratroops to evacuate Zimzim Rest Camp and present themselves at the docks in Algiers by early afternoon. Full battle order, the notice said, and there were no airstrips in the dockyard. So it was a trip by sea.

The men of the outfit ate their breakfast like wolves. They were behaving as if it would be their last good meal in North Africa.

Sergeant Johnson, and his friends newly promoted to corporals were all clustered round one end of a long table. Other buddies were just a little further along. Pongo Smith, for once, showed a sense of humour.

He remarked: 'I wouldn't eat too much of that fat bacon if I was you, Ginger, especially if you're prone to seasickness. Might make you look a bit soft in front of the matelots, you know.'

Potts slowed up and began to feel uneasy over his eating for the first time since the meal began. 'You really think it'll be rough, Pongo?'

'To a fellow with a queasy stomach it always seems rough,' Smith added, with a general wink up the table.

Potts started to pick at his food. So did several of the others. It was one thing to parachute out of the sky onto the scrub-grown side of a hill, and another thing entirely to make a sea voyage and then be expected to fight at the end of it.

'Where do you blokes reckon we're goin' then?' Lofty Wright wanted to know.

This question was being bandied about all over the dining hall. No wonder it stilled tongues and caused eating irons to be used more quietly. Those who usually had an opinion to offer became the focus of the eyes of others.

'What do you think, Sarge?' Potts asked, as he pushed away the fried part of his breakfast.

'Just because I've got an extra stripe, mate, don't think Eisenhower an' them other brass 'ats take me into their confidence. If you want me to guess, I will do, though. I say we're goin' to Pantellaria. An' don't ask me why, 'cause this meal is very important to me.'

'What's Pantellaria then?' Pongo wanted to know. 'Sounds like a pantomime to me.'

'Maybe it is. It's a useful small island between Sicily and Tunisia, this side of Malta,' Nick explained.

'You think we might be goin' there, Nick?' Potts persisted.

'Could be,' Nick mumbled. 'On the other hand, there's another island bigger than that one and closer in to the coast of Tunisia. We might be going to occupy that, or again it might be Lampedusa or Linosa. Plenty of islands in the Med.'

'What if it isn't an island at all?' Jock Pawson suggested.

'Go on, Jock, tell us your theory,' Lofty prompted.

'I don't see why it shouldn't be on the mainland of Tunisia, behind the German lines,' the Scot explained. 'After all, Monty must be nearly here by now. It's time we made a show of some sort. If we're not careful the history books will say the Eighth cleared North Africa on their own!'

'Here, hold on a minute, Jock,' Potts protested. 'Our blokes an' the Yanks aren't doin' all that bad. We haven't got as many troops in the field as what people think. An' the French are not as well equipped as we are!'

'An' don't forget the weather, an' all!' Johnson put in. 'It isn't like chasin' Rommel across nice flat warm sand!'

Somebody poured the sergeant a fresh cup of tea, and in so doing finished a discussion which had become an argument about the fortunes of war.

★ ★ ★

A brief air raid delayed the line up of troops on the jetty in Algiers harbour. According to the Navy it was 1615 hours when the first paratrooper walked across the destroyer's gangway and clambered down a metal ladder to his temporary quarters for the journey.

Only two ships had been detailed off to

take the Red Devils, and this gave them further cause for speculation. No support from other sections of the Army. What could that mean? If the naval personnel knew what it was all about, they kept the secret to themselves as the men with the bulging Everest packs filed aboard in splendid order.

The second of the two vessels was an L.C.T.; a tank landing craft. There were no tanks to be taken aboard, of course, and an awning had been rigged across the top of the well deck where the iron-clads were usually housed.

When Captain Burns' voice started to give orders, the paras in the L.C.T. began to sort themselves out. Taking passage in the blunt-bowed flat-bottomed landing craft were three of the sections of B troop. These were Section One, of sappers, and Sections Two and Three of parachuting infantry. The quarters on a landing craft are essentially small. As this one carried two officers and they had to share a small room just big enough to hold two bunks, several of the officers connected with the troop were taking passage aboard the destroyer. Apart from Captain Burns, there was only Lieutenant Maine, Canadian subaltern in charge of the sappers.

During the parachute training, Harvey Maine had developed a certain tension in dropping from the skies by silk. As soon as he knew they were not flying to their next objecttive, his relief knew no bounds and he never ceased to talk all day. Johnson, Potts and the other old comrades listened to the subaltern sounding off as they mustered on board, and Nick was the object of many sympathetic glances.

Promptly at 1700 hours, the destroyer and the landing craft cast off and slipped away from the harbour walls. Idling naval and army personnel gave them a cheer and there was the customary saluting of flags between ship and shore, and ship and ship. Soon they had cleared the harbour bar, and the bows were pointing towards the east.

'Well, that kills one rumour,' Nick remarked. 'We aren't going home for long leave, unless it's via China and Japan!'

Speculation broke out afresh in the

packed well deck. The passengers stayed noisy until a throat clearing was magnified over a loud hailer.

'Do you hear there? This is the skipper speaking. Make sure you are in a spot where you can hear well because Captain Burns has asked me to inform you where you are heading for.'

Almost half a minute elapsed before Lieutenant Jim Middlewood, R.N.V.R., made his short, deflating speech. The skipper was a plump, fair bearded man in a soiled reefer and a peaked cap which had very little shape beyond the peak.

'On behalf of the crew of L.C.T. 17A I'd like to welcome officers and men of the Red Devils on board. As to your destination, I won't keep you in suspense. For us this is a routine run to Bone, a small port some fifty miles this side of the Tunisian border. I think you will be moved from there into the hills to bolster up the British, American and French troops who are already engaged.

'Unfortunately, we can't offer you first class facilities. Our quarters are cramped for the fourteen of us who run this vessel, but we will do anything we can to make life easy for you. Of late, we haven't had much trouble from Axis naval forces, but it would be wrong to assume there aren't any about.

'I hope for your sakes we have a quiet trip. You can expect to reach Bone about dawn the day after tomorrow. That's all.'

So finally the speculation as to the destination was ended. All that this trip amounted to was a return to everyday fighting as infantrymen in the hills west and south-west of the vital part of the country.

In the warmth under the awning, men began to relax, yawn, smoke and make themselves at home. For a time, they turned away from the faces of their friends which they would see all the time once they reached the mountains. Instead, they turned to the naval men, envying them their pleasant tan and the apparently unconcerned attitude which went with everything they did.

Lieutenant Middlewood threw his narrow compact bridge open to both officers and any N.C.O.'s who wanted to look round it. He would also have permitted the ordinary privates, except that there was no room. The privates were allowed out of the hold. They wandered around the quarterdeck and the narrow walks down beside the guardrails.

For a time, Johnson, Potts and Nick stood right over the bows and watched the buffeting waves creaming away from the blunt bows. They looked aft, beyond the wheelhouse and the bridge, and felt the struggle which any blunt-bowed craft has in a sea of any strength.

About half an hour elapsed during which the trio studied the destroyer about half a cable's length on the port beam. They waved to opposite numbers walking the slim ocean grey-hound's decks and remarked how it pitched and tossed from bow to stern.

Shortly after that, as the swell of the sea appeared to grow, those with the queasy stomachs started to feel uneasy. Nick's officer, who had been on the bridge talking loudly for about forty minutes, suddenly turned green and left without so much as a good-bye. Scouse and Nick laughed, but Potts, who was not feeling very steady, couldn't manage a grin.

Presently, Johnson began to get bored. He suggested to Potts a game of cards, and, thinking the sickening sensation would be felt less down below, Ginger hurriedly agreed. Nick, who did not play cards, suggested a later meeting. He wandered aft, alone, and found himself alongside of a lanky able seaman with short wavy hair, bulbous eyes and rather fleshy lips.

Able Seaman Tom Drigg, it transpired, came from Dalton, a town not far from Nick's birthplace. They talked about faces and places they knew back home while Drigg rubbed out his dirty clothing in a dhobeying bucket. Officially, he was the duty pom-pom gunner, but because so much monotonous time was wasted standing by the gun, many obvious chores such as laundering clothes were carried out there.

Nick was just warming to a discussion on walking and cycling in the Lake District when a bell sounded off, and Drigg was relieved of his duty by another rating. The First Dog Watch was at an end.

Nick wandered about some more, and marvelled at the way his stomach was putting up with the ship's motion. He found himself wondering for perhaps the fiftieth time what his officer would be like in action. Harvey Maine's accent pervaded every conversation even when he didn't shout, because of the unusualness of the accent. To most of the men in his section, it was an American accent; one like they had heard on the films.

Maine was undoubtedly a strong man. He had big shoulders and arms, as though at one time he might have been a lumberjack. He was also quite handsome, having green eyes and well-groomed fair hair. At that time, however, he was vomiting into the wake and narrowly missing the flapping ensign.

A.B. Drigg reappeared on duty at eight in the evening to keep the First Watch until midnight. On that occasion, he pushed his dhobeying bucket on one side and thrust his hands deep into the pockets of his duffle. He started to open up, and soon he was talking about his conquests in one port and another.

Nick listened with tolerance, and tried to work him round to another topic, but the seaman was proud of his apparent power over unattached women. The sun was just beginning to dip in the west when Nick turned the other's mind to convoy runs up and down the Mediterranean coast.

Drigg handed him a home-rolled cigarette. 'Between Algiers and Bone it's pretty quiet these days, but at one time we didn't 'ave it all our own way. Running between Mersa an' Tobruk when Rommel laid siege to the port, now them were the days! A thirty-three hours run it was, with E-boats after your blood sometimes, an' air raids an' a big gun called Long Tom that used to pump 'orrible great shells at you just as you were gettin' near 'arbour. Why at one time the 'arbour at Tobruk was full of wrecks. All you could see were the masts of sunken ships sticking out of the drink all over the place.'

Nick's attention wandered as the L-class destroyer tired of the eight knot maximum speed imposed upon her by the landing craft and made a half circle round behind them.

'How about aircraft an' subs?' Nick asked.

Drigg shrugged. 'Oh well, we got radar an' asdic in the ships what 'ave refitted. In these crates we've got our strengths an' weaknesses same as any other.'

Nick's attention stayed on the destroyer. With his arms resting on the guardrail he followed it with his eyes. At the end of its half circle, the destroyer went about and started back again. It had reached a point on the port quarter when the sapper corporal's interest intensified.

'I say, Tom, what does the track of a torpedo look like? It must be something you can't forget once you've seen it!'

'Oh, it's easy enough to pick out, mate. It makes a long straight wake and the white water gradually spreads the further back you look!'

Nick's lips dried out. He had seen such a track of white water appear behind the destroyer as it sped back into position on the port beam. The white track came straight for the landing craft as though it was magnetized.

Suddenly the sapper found his voice. He turned to the bridge and cupped his hands. '*Torpedo on the port quarter, sir!*'

Drigg almost fell out of the pom-pom gun harness. There was a rush of feet to the port side of the vessel as those who had the responsibility strove to get further essential information before it was too late.

The Skipper yelled: 'Stand by, Swain!'

In the wheelhouse, the cox'n licked his lips and hoped he would have time to make a worthwhile manoeuvre. He had no illusions as to L.C.T. 17A's fate if the torpedo struck her.

'Hard aport!' Middlewood yelled.

He put everything he had into the shout and somehow he kept out the despair he felt, because he knew beyond a shadow of doubt that the blunt bows would not answer fast enough to swing her clear. Neither was it any use to call down below for maximum revs. The boat was almost full out as it was, and it took a few seconds for the P.O. Motor Mechanic to make the increase.

The extended white line of foam came straight for the port quarter. Young Richard Mullen, the First Lieutenant, bellowed into a voice-pipe. His clipped public school accent sounded very fulsome in the circumstances.

''Ware torpedo! Clear the messdecks!'

Every man's stomach knotted up as he lived through the last vital seconds before the torpedo's warhead struck the thin plates of the craft. The passengers soon got the impression that the buffeting was overdue. They did not relax, however, thinking in their ignorance that an explosion in water perhaps took a little time to manifest itself.

The overdueness dragged to half a minute. Nick forced his head round to see how Drigg was behaving. The able seaman was pointing with a shaking hand to the white track, which was still extending on the other side of the vessel.

'It's not possible,' Nick muttered.

Drigg nodded hard, but did not have the use of his tongue. Meanwhile the destroyer flashed an urgent signal by Aldis Lamp and increased her speed to a good thirty knots. She leapt away from the ship she was escorting in the direction from which the track had come. For a few crazy moments, Nick thought she was going in the wrong direction, and then he got his thinking straight.

She was going to the source of the torpedo, the U-boat which had fired it. They could still hear the clanging of her engine-room telegraph on the open bridge when she hove to and prepared to drop her first salvo of depth charges.

This was one run not to be written off as uneventful.

11

Altogether H.M.S. *Livid*, the destroyer, made three runs across the place where the U-boat was thought to be skulking with her machinery silenced to avoid making noises. Each run ended with six canisters of amatol, known as depth charges, somersaulting through the air after leaving the throwers on the stern end of the vessel.

They hit the water and plunged to a preset depth before exploding. At the end of each run, the surface ship used its instruments in an effort to find out if the submarine had started up its motors in an attempt to slip away. They heard no sound at all.

Subsequent runs were made at varying depths in a calculated attempt to secure a kill. After the third run, a lookout spotted a small slick of oil on the surface and one or two small personal items of seamen's gear. The captain, however, was a veteran sub-hunter and he was far from convinced that the pressure hull of the submarine had been breached. He thought it was just as likely that the oil and the objects had been deliberately sent up to the surface to make the attacker think the undersea ship was doomed.

The commanding officer thought about it for a long minute, and then decided to stop hunting. He gave the order for the depth charge party to secure the remaining canisters, and turned his ship to follow the landing craft. During the time when they had been hunting the L.C.T. had opened a gap between them of almost four miles.

As the light was going and the landing craft was vulnerable, the destroyer had to get back to station. An escort could not do its duty unless it was within a reasonably close distance of its charge.

The crew and the passengers aboard the landing craft lined the rails, apart from duty men, and watched the hunter coming back to station with a huge white bow wave splitting away from her knife bows. By that time, Able Seaman Drigg had recovered his poise after dropping one of Nick's precious tailor-made cigarettes overboard.

Drigg was sufficiently recovered to manage a chuckle. 'Well, townie, as the Skipper said over the blower just now, it ain't everybody who can say they've taken passage in a vessel when a tinfish 'as passed right underneath an' come up the other side.

'You could 'ave learned a lot from that experience, if you was wide awake. First off, we didn't 'ave enough speed to run out of the way of the 'fish. Secondly, the bows are too blunt for 'er to be swung aside in time. But, an' it's a big but, we only draw about eight feet in ordinary times, an' when a tinfish is set to go through the 'ogwash a bit low it means that it goes right underneath us an' up the other side without doin' any trouble. Remember 'ow I told you even a vessel like this 'as its points.'

Nick grinned at Drigg's relief and his powers of speech when the heat was off. He said shrewdly: 'I suppose the tin-fish was set to hit the destroyer, low in the water. An' they missed her, and we weren't low enough, eh?'

Drigg confirmed this. They talked on for another fifteen minutes during which the shoreline vanished into darkness and the upper works of the destroyer faded above her phosphorescent waterline. Nick was the one to break off the conversation and go down below. His bed roll was calling.

Inevitably, the messdeck and the hold or well deck became stuffy with so many bodies sharing it, but the men using the limited facilities had all been in the armed forces for several years and they put up with the lack of space and amenities with good-natured tolerance.

The night became cool, so that none of the duty hands stayed above decks without their duffle-coats on. The same night air prevented passengers from putting down their bed rolls on the upper deck, or, indeed on the upper side of the canvas awning.

Dawn cracked the dark dome of the sky towards the east and slowly and without apparent effort the darkness was converted into greyness which was chased away in the form of shadows. Shortly before seven a.m. a twenty-year-old lookout with a back sliding nose and ears like wind scoops detected alien noises in the sky.

'Alarm port!' he bellowed hoarsely. 'Planes on the port bow!'

The Skipper tripped over the top step of the bridge ladder and stumbled into his First Lieutenant. 'Hell's bells, Number One, before this trip is over I'll begin to think there's something very special about seaborne paratroops! What the hell has Goering got in store for us now?'

'Just a couple of Stukas, sir. Look as if they've been in mothballs since last we were attacked! Here they come, right from where the sun would be if it were visible. Doesn't it gall you when you think about the hour they must have risen on Sicily or Sardinia simply to come and do this to us?'

Middlewood chuckled at his junior's droll way of describing the situation. 'Leave the manœuvring to me and aim that machine-gun at them if you feel like it!'

Sub-Lieutenant Mullen was a thin-featured likeable young fellow. His public school accent endeared him to the lower deck rather than accentuated the difference between his and their education. Although there were small dark rings round his eyes, he almost clicked his heels in delight.

'Yes, sir!'

While bleary-eyed men in gum boots thumped about the deck, Mullen hastily donned his tin hat and anti-flash gear. He raised himself on tiptoe and peered further aft to the pom-pom platforms. Several of the hands were quite expert with the two-barrelled pom-poms, and usually there was a rush to man them.

On this occasion, Drigg was on the port gun, having been on watch from four o'clock. A small round-faced lad with dark curly hair, Taff Jones, had made it to the starboard weapon.

'Two Stukas, lads. Both pilots have been out of their flea pits for longer than some of you, so don't let them put anything over on you!'

Middlewood called for maximum engine

revolutions and fondled the rim of his binnacle while he waited for the action to develop. In the wheelhouse, Petty Officer Wilkins, a native of Hull, locked the wheel with an arm through the spokes. He glanced down at the photograph of his petite wife, pinned to the bulkhead, and surreptitiously smoothed his magnificent Captain Kettle beard and moustache.

'Here we go again, girl,' he murmured, and turned his muttering into the tune and words of a comic song.

For a time, it was not at all certain where the attack was going to develop. The only thing the naval personnel were at all sure about was the type of aircraft, and the fact that they were flying at a particularly low altitude.

Sub-Lieutenant Mullen only cursed when they were in action. He cursed on this occasion because he thought the gunners on board the destroyer were going to have all the fun. Both Stukas headed towards the faster, better-armed vessel, but at the last second the rearmost plane turned to port and came diving towards the landing craft.

Nick Burrows, who was scrambling up a ladder with sleep in his eyes, heard Mullen's oath bitten off short. He also heard the Skipper quietly underlining the fact that the gunners would be needed in a few seconds. Nick crouched double, after emerging from a deck hatch. He rushed to the rear of the superstructure, and hoped to see most of the action from there without getting in the way of any flying metal.

'Watch it!' Middlewood yelled.

During the course of many actions of this type, he had developed a facility which was almost uncanny for knowing when a pilot or air gunner was about to open up on them.

Several seconds before the landing craft gunners cut loose, the destroyer was in action. A four-inch gun, several Oerlikons and two machine-guns threw a telling fusillade of explosives towards the first fighter bomber which was seeking to rake their pitching decks with machine-gun bullets.

Two men were hit by the plane's bullets, and then the counter fire began to have an effect. Nick, crouched low and with his teeth clenched, forced his attention away from the plane which was bearing down upon the L.C.T., and glanced across to the destroyer. Plane and ship converged very rapidly. The plane appeared to be magnetizing its own special quota of shells and bullets from the ship.

Bullets ripped at it all round the perspex of the cockpit and the wing roots, and still it went on, although its pilot had perforce to ease back his control column to miss the worst of the flying lead. The Stuka sailed over the top of the mast, having caused no further damage than a small hole or two in armour plating and wounding two men. The attacker climbed the sky, banking as it did so, intent on a second attack.

Nick caught glimpses of the grim-faced pilot of the second plane as he squeezed the button of his machine-guns at maximum range. Suddenly, the young officer on the bridge was pouring a counter stream at the plane, and the deck plates vibrated as Drigg led his mate on the starboard side into action on the pom-poms.

'*Everybody down!*'

Somehow the Skipper's shouted warning came through the general cacophony of sound as the Stuka thundered in and over the ship with scarcely a fathom to spare when it cleared the mast. The pom-pom gunners recovered quickly; Drigg sent a burst after the plane as it climbed astern.

The crews and passengers waited in an agony of tension as the aerial attackers banked round and came in again. For some reason best known to themselves, they swopped targets. And the second attack was about to be delivered from astern. At once, the destroyer started to zigzag, and her stern end gunners were primed to fend off the new attack. The Stuka roared down onto them, and when it was still a few hundred feet away, two small bombs were released. Down they came, plummeting apparently straight for the vessel. The commanding officer ordered a sharp turn to starboard and suddenly the four-inch guns were firing and belching brief red flames.

The pilot started to pull out early, being content to let his bombs do his work. The Oerlikons and four-inch guns followed him and one shell missed his fuselage by less than a yard. He pulled back his stick and kicked over his rudder, taking maximum evasive action.

The second plane was well into its dive when the first bombs fell. A huge gout of water climbed skyward some twenty feet clear of the destroyer's port quarter, and the second explosion was fifty yards away. The rat-a-tat thump of the landing craft's pom-poms made the teeth of the nearest personnel judder. They hung on, and the gunners adjusted their aim by swinging on the harness as the bombs came away.

The starboard gun almost ringed the perspex of the cockpit and caused the pilot to lose concentration. Before he had recovered himself and shifted his controls a shell from the port side weapon had buried itself in the starboard wing roots. A small area started to smoke, and the naval men were yelling with triumph when the bombs smacked down into the sea within seconds of each other.

One gout was thirty feet off the starboard bow and the other was twenty feet to port. The heavy bow of the vessel lifted a few feet out of the water and solemnly smacked the surface again. Lieutenant Middlewood and Sub-Lieutenant Mullen faced each other and listened most carefully. One of them was draped over the binnacle and the other was on his knees.

Nobody shouted up from the well deck to say that the big bow door had sprung a leak. Gradually, that kind of anxiety faded. The Stuka which had just attacked them developed a long plume of smoke. Very slowly and gradually it lost height as it went away in the direction from which it had appeared. The other plane flew on and away. Eventually Drigg's victim suffered an explosion. A part of the wing came away, and the aircraft went into the sea, spinning like a sycamore seed.

By that time, the defenders had recovered and the destroyer C.O. had signalled his congratulations over the 'kill.'

Later in the day, *Luftwaffe* planes came

again, but the Allies were able to rush a few Spitfires into the area to give the two ships protection. Daylight on that second day out seemed reluctant to fade, but eventually it did, and round about dawn the morning after the word went round that they were putting in to Bone.

The day had started on fine drizzle, but many paratroopers braved the elements to get their first glimpse of shore. Under a haze of rain and distant storm clouds, the small port of Bone looked anything but attractive. There were masts sticking out of the harbour waters in great profusion. Devastated railway trucks and twisted lines populated jetties which had had huge holes blasted out of the concrete.

The waters of the harbour were a rich muddy colour and they smelled unpleasantly. To Nick Burrows, a product of a shipyard town, the sights, sounds and smells were utterly demoralizing.

12

Within half an hour, the sun was up and the garrison of Bone had come down to the jetty to help unload the ships in the least possible time. Able Seaman Drigg and others held a shouted conversation with harbour seamen in khaki as the unloading proceeded. Someone told the local boys how Drigg had scored a 'kill' and after that the voices were raised in greater excitement.

Dunstable and his two troop commanders took their leave of the naval companies and marched their men out of the dockyard into the town which was in slightly better repair than the docks.

Some of Drigg's earlier talk about the way Tobruk had been shelled and bombed made Nick wonder. Bone had all the appearance of being as roughly handled as the port further east, and yet Drigg had not mentioned the obvious damage there. Nick decided that he had

199

seen the debris and the wrecks so often that he no longer saw them.

Soon the harbour was out of sight, and the marching party was halted at an old draughty building. They were stood at ease for five minutes and then taken inside to sit at long wooden tables which were still covered in dust from the last air raid. The men tired of waiting for the overdue breakfast, and soon the whole of the great room was filled with conversations, most of which never were finished.

Nick found himself staring down at the table top in front of him. He found a spot where some other traveller had earlier carved a heart on the top with two sets of initials. *H.B. loves K.B.* He started to try and think of a name for the initials K.B. Katherine . . . Kate. Both had surnames starting with the same letter. Of course, if the lovesick soldier happened to be married, that accounted for the similar surname initials. Otherwise, the surnames might be as different as Black and Billingsgate. His mouth was forming into a crooked smile when it occurred to him that one set of initials were exactly the same as those of his brother. *Harry Burrows*.

His mind slid away from the initials and instead groped for his brother. He couldn't remember exactly what the officer had said back there in Zimzim. 'See you somewhere around Medjez . . . ' had it been. He thought it had. So Harry was somewhere up there ahead. He had probably eaten food off this table, or one like it, on the way.

Harry in the mountains west of Tunis! That was good. Good for Nick, if he could locate him, which would be exceedingly difficult. And good for the British Army in general because Harry was a first class man in and around mountains!

Nick ate two overcooked sausages without being aware of it while his mind toyed with the intriguing possibility of seeing Harry. Harry who was big, solid, dependable and entirely unflappable. His mind passed from Harry to the terrain in which they were going to fight.

There were three gaps in the hills west of Tunis. Furthest north was the valley of the River Sedjenane. Next was the River Medjerda valley, and the third was the pass of Pont du Fahs. Almost certainly Harry's outfit had to be engaged somewhere near or actually in the hills around those valleys.

He wondered what the odds were of bumping into him. At the time, it never occurred to him that either one or the other of them might become casualties before they had the chance to meet. Nick was a pessimist at times, but not in matters connected with action and death. He grinned with his mouth full as he envisaged his older brother curling his tongue round names like Mateur, Protville, Goubellat and Enfidaville. Harry was a mighty smart fellow in many ways. No doubt he would be able to base geography lessons around his wartime travels when he got home!

Lofty Wright, sitting opposite, said: 'If you can't swallow that 'orrible banger, Nick, spit it out. I promise I won't look.'

The conversation engulfed Nick. He was drawn into the banalities of the others, and the outfit remained cheerful until they heard lorries pulling up outside; after that, their minds were filled with new speculation. Some had expected to go on from Bone by rail, but these three ton open-backed Chevrolets seemed to indicate the whole journey by road — and goat track, as some wag observed.

After the meal, they packed their kit into the lorries and were then given a couple of hours to stretch their legs and take a look round the town before the commencement of the journey. There was little to buy in the shops, and although the French population turned out to be friendly there was little time to get acquainted with them.

Bone, to the Red Devils, was merely a transit camp, and the men of Captain Burns' B Troop were glad when the eight Chevrolets finally rolled out of Algeria's port furthest east and proceeded up the coast road towards the region of trouble.

Distantly to the north they caught sight of a convoy, hull down on the horizon, making its way in leisurely fashion to Malta, and perhaps beyond. Somebody produced a pair of binoculars, and Nick and his sapper section spent a speculative ten minutes trying to figure out what sort of stores or equipment were carried in the crates stacked on the freighters' decks. There was friendly argument, too, about the identity of the fleet carrier which was part of the escort. Nick knew that it was one of the *Indomitable* class, two of which had been built in his home-town, but he could not figure which of the class it was. Had he been called upon to gamble, he would have named the *Illustri-ous*, but his interest waned, like that of the other sappers as the trucks left the coast road and proceeded almost due south towards the glowering hills and the clouds, black with menace, gently hovering over them.

The downpouring rain hastened the onrush of darkness that night and the slow meandering mountain roads which led towards Souk-el-Arba were soon a dripping slimy mess which made it difficult for the heavy tyres to take a firm grip. The drivers battled on, snug in their cabs, with the windscreen wipers working incessantly in front of their faces. In the rear of the

Chevs, things were different. Every possible item of clothing which might keep out a bit of the rain was donned or draped over the occupants, and to no avail.

It was persistent, heavy, wetting rain and its chilling drops worked their way through the clothing of all the troops, gradually lowering their morale, their body warmth and their confidence in the Army as a worthwhile way of seeing the world. Water swished about on the boards under their booted feet, and nothing, nothing at all happened to improve their morale. They were jolted and jarred. Their backs developed red bruises where the wet clothing had been pressed into them by the sides of the vehicle.

Every Chev was the same. The one carrying the sappers was fourth in line. From time to time, its headlights picked out the one ahead, and it, in its turn, was caught by the lights of number five. Nick was hemmed in by three sappers who were new to the Red Devils. Their names were Fred Horsfall, Jake Shaw, and Billy Thomas. Fred answered to 'Red' because his hair was sandy. He was a freckled optimist, who had worked on the Black-pool Golden Mile, keeping the machines in order. Jake Shaw was an ex-police constable from Wigan. He had worked in an engineering shop before joining the force, and his previous experience had stood him in good stead when he insisted on joining up and picking his own branch of the services. The third of this group of friends was a Welsh Lancastrian with fair wavy hair. Billy Thomas was his name. He claimed to have once worked on the Llanberis-Snowdon railway, but nobody could ever be sure that he was speaking the truth about it.

After the Chev had lurched and slithered round one of many bends and gradually picked up speed again, Jake Shaw, the ex-policeman, suddenly jerked to his feet. He threw his arms wide and scattered the water off his gas cape.

'Why the hell did we have to come *this* way?' he shouted. 'I got my red beret because I wanted to jump!'

Next, he yawned and belched and finally slumped back in his seat with a loud groan. He was full-faced and possessed a wide mouth, the outer corners of which turned down. But it soon became apparent that he was not as downcast as he sounded.

Horsfall and Thomas started to giggle, in spite of the cold, and thus encouraged, Shaw cleared his throat and started to improvize.

'Who'd be a copper on a night like this, eh? Who'd volunteer for a bit of traffic duty in a downpour like this? Give me Manchester any day, and better still, Wigan!'

He caught a glint in a 'foreign' eye. 'Come to London and join the You Know What police force, that's what they say when they want to coax a few northern lads down to the Big Smoke. I went once. Never again. All the way to Wembley in civvies. I should have been on duty. That way I could have seen the game. I can see you're wondering if it was a fine day. Well, it was, I'll grant you that.

'It was goin' to Wembley finally made me want to learn to swim. You see, I joined this queue outside. I made sure it must be a fish an' chip queue, you see.

Then, too late, I found it led to a toilet. There was no going back by then. I didn't want to go, either. But believe you me it was deeper in there than high tide under Wigan pier. I've never been so scared in all my life. I didn't mind the paddlin' so much, but it was me boots, you see. They were my service boots, and they got such a soaking they shrunk eventually. I had no end of trouble with them before we got home.

'And to cap it all, our team lost. And we had the best away record in England.' Suddenly he seemed to run out of steam. He looked down at his boots and remarked: 'I'll be interested to see if these boots can take as much punishment as police footwear.'

Thirty seconds of silence ensued, and suddenly the rest of the sappers, who had been pretending to sleep, burst out into laughter and to some small extent resuscitated themselves. Nick perceived that life, during the boring lulls, might not be as insufferable as he had anticipated.

★ ★ ★

The rain never abated and a transit camp absorbed them in the cold light of early morning. They were fed and allowed to wander at will through cultivated land and olive groves rooted in mud. Brief, uncomfortable periods of sleep followed, during which the Chevrolets went back to the coast.

In place of the Chevs were bigger troop-carrying vehicles, the canvas covers of which kept out the rain, but there were still trials like cramped limbs to be suffered, and having too many bodies in too little space.

During the next hilly trip, explosives began to land on the road ahead. One after another the trucks pulled up suddenly. The driver and Captain Burns went forward with torches after all the vehicles had dowsed their lights. It was as well they did. A couple of small bombs, which might have come from mortars, had made small craters in the road.

Neither hole was big enough to throw a vehicle on its own, but they had rapidly filled with water, and the muddy soil around them had crumbled away. Volunteers from the first truck got down with shovels and filled them in. The rest waited, under cover, but shivering.

Soon, the first lorry was away, but when the rest tried they found they were on a steeper incline, and that it was necessary to get out and push to stop the wheels from spraying mud in all directions and further eroding the track. One lorry load of men could not cope with the weight of their vehicle. Two lorry loads, helped out by ropes and sacks, finally did achieve some success in getting the vehicles started upwards again. Every truck except the first one waited until the rest were moving.

The weary men, back in the seats, felt that they had only been asleep for a half hour when the vehicles stopped again and they heard the order to debus. Dawn in the east looked as unprepossessing as ever in that Tunisian winter sky, but this was the end of the journey.

Men and equipment were stripped out. They moved off the road and started to make a camp, while some of their number found suitable places well in the bushes and heather to hide the vehicles. There were tents to be rigged, ditches to be dug and trenches also.

It was while he and his men were rigging barbed wire that Nick's mind went back to the two craters in the road. He could not remember anyone having taken shelter from the explosives, or, indeed, waiting for the offensive to desist. He decided that the top ranking officers must have been as fatigued as the men, and that they had not bothered to think about the source of the trouble.

Sapper Shaw brought his mind back to the present. 'I suppose in theory we ought to give as our address on letters 'Somewhere in Tunisia,' Corp. You got any bright ideas what I could buy my wife as a souvenir of this place?'

At that time of the morning, Nick was completely out of ideas and annoyed with himself because of it. He said: 'Ask me when breakfast is finished, Jake.' Shaw took him at his word, but he never got round to asking because an artillery bombardment curtailed the meal.

13

The Red Devils had been pushed back into the fighting line as an extra fighting force of first class infantry. Already dug in along the extended British salient which overlooked two of the valley approaches to Tunis and the other towns and ports in the north were several famous regiments. At least three regiments of Guards were represented in the fierce fighting for the last German-held territory in Africa. One of them won the nickname of the 'plumbers' because of the number of times they were moved about to plug gaps in the British lines.

Major Dunstable's men were towards the south of the sector.

All of them were in the hills near to the town of Bou Arada which was along the route of the pass of Pont du Fahs. Neither side controlled the valley, at least not by having troops down there in it; but the Allies had virtual control because they had the upper hand in the heights around it.

Their numbers were not excessive although efforts had been made to increase their strength throughout the bitter months of December and January. Rommel's retreat over sixteen hundred miles into the Gabes gap had been masterly. Once he had joined forces with the troops already established in Tunisia, he started to make his presence felt. All the way through Libya and Tripolitania he had been collecting troops left behind to guard his lines of communication and man his workshops. He had them all with him when he joined the defensive ring in Tunisia and began to fight a delaying war to keep the Allies from making an early invasion of Europe.

Before the arrival of the Red Devils, the Germans had made a useful thrust through the central part of the contested ground. Tanks and artillery made short, unheralded advances rendering life decidedly unpleasant for the men who hoped to hold the muddy hills until the balance of war changed.

The German artillery shifted its target quite regularly, and also moved its position as the Allied air forces probed to find them, but the paratroops began to look thoughtful when on three days running their part of the salient received a trouncing by shells. In other terrain, shelling was used to soften up the opposition before an attempted advance. But how could the Boche hope to make an advance against crack troops who held the heights?

Nick was one of those who reasoned in this way, and like the others he was soon to find out.

One morning when the new Allied airstrips further west were still shrouded in mist, the guns of the British positions further north began to bark at a high angle. For a time, Dunstable's men were puzzled, and then, quite suddenly, everything became clear.

German planes were coming down from the north-east. Not the ordinary fighters, or fighter-bombers who usually penetrated the fastnesses before making off again. These were towing planes with powerful engines; very airworthy, but not particularly fast; which said volumes for their pilots, who had to hang on and take everything that was slung at them until such time as the gliders, on tow behind them, were pointed at the landing slopes and also almost there.

The word was passed around the saddle in the hills which the Red Devils commanded. Brens were aimed at the towing planes in an effort to get them to drop their towing ropes before the gliders were in position. On they came, through a veritable sea of flak. Six gallant pilots, death and glory boys to a man. Although they were expert pilots, they could not use their controls to jinx about without the great danger of capsizing the gliders which were carrying crack troops, hoping to capture the heights from the British.

As the hostile fire from the hills built up, and British artillery began to get their range, two of the pilots succumbed to nerves. One cast his tow rope clear and dived rather recklessly down the valley, heading south-west. Before he managed to pull clear again, the artillery riddled his machine with the inevitable result that he ended his days against a hillside. His machine flamed for a half hour before the drizzle put it out.

The second plane to drop its tow banked steeply and almost stood on its starboard wing before concentrated fire from further up the salient riddled its undercarriage and tail and prevented its safe return.

The first glider landed rather heavily on the road through the pass. The troopers were slow to spill out, and when they did so, the artillery bracketed them and gradually reduced them to a litter of bodies. The travellers in the second sail plane were more fortunate as to their landing place. This one also landed heavily. The first six men out of it were riddled, but others, emerging at a different spot, began to fire back and spread themselves out on the slope behind the pinnacle of high mountainous rock which dominated the hill saddle like a pommel, or saddle horn.

The men of B Troop, dug in at the pinnacle end, made desperate efforts to eliminate these men before the other gliders landed and made life more complicated. Three-quarters of the troopers were out of the second glider before its tail was hit by a mortar bomb. Subsequently it caught fire, and men who went back to assist their comrades failed to survive the hostile fire.

After that, a glider was landing on the slopes around the pinnacle about every three minutes. Three landed in this way, the while most of the paratroops were engaged behind their weapons, the sixth and last glider skimmed the edge of the saddle and came in from the north-west to land almost in the middle of the saddle and just to one side of the first aid tent.

Before it grounded itself properly, guns were firing from its open ports and several men around the perimeter of the saddle had fallen to the ground with bullets in their backs.

Oddly enough, the glider made its entry when Major Dunstable, his two Captains, the two Sapper subalterns, and the Sapper sections of the two troops were in close conclave near the casualty tent.

Lieutenant Maine was the first to see it coming. His green eyes flashed and he pointed, cutting short Dunstable's instructions.

'My Section, grip your weapons an' move round the Red Cross tent!' he bellowed.

Dunstable and his two captains threw themselves towards the tent, while the other section, encouraged by its equally enthusiastic officer, crouched low and went the other way, actually passing under the nose of the sail plane just before it touched down. German Schmeissers raked the tent, and those who were not in it spent a second or two hoping their senior officers were not standing up in there.

The glider lurched to a halt some fifty yards beyond the tent. Its starboard wing made contact with the ground and a door opened. An arm came out and tossed a stick grenade to discourage the sappers hurrying to the spot. Both sections fell flat, and luckily, none of them were hit. Up they came, and on they went again.

For Maine's outfit, Sapper Shaw threw

a grenade which burst against the starboard wing and took three Germans out of their stride. Others pitched over them, and the weapons of Nick, Thomas, Horsfall and others ripped into them. And still the door spewed more men in grey uniforms.

Something heavier than Stens was needed to stop them.

Maine tossed two grenades from a kneeling position. One hit the dead pile, and the other burst over the fuselage doing little damage. While he was still busy, Nick waved some of the men forward, and thrilled at the way they responded. Maine opened his mouth to shout something after them, and then thought better of it. He swung his arm like a bowler does to loosen up before an over at cricket.

He was almost ready to release another grenade when a bullet, one of a small burst from a glider port, hit him squarely in the forehead. The pin was out of the explosive, but his fingers never parted with it. Fortunately, no one else was close enough to die with the officer when the explosion blasted his body.

On the port side of the plane, the other section made a lot of progress and then suddenly found themselves being decimated by cunning Germans who were using their wits to try and get out and start a pocket of resistance. Nick waved his men flat with the ground as paras of A Troop on the perimeter turned their weapons inwards and supported the struggling sappers.

Two Brens, worked by expert marksmen, cut down on the Germans the moment they tried to break out of the mound of dead down the starboard side. Nick waited for three minutes. He waved his men forward again, but this time crawling. Shaw was within five yards of the wall of dead when he lobbed a grenade over it. The cries from the other side left no doubt about its efficacy.

Meanwhile, Billy Thomas, Red Horsfall and Nick crawled towards the fuselage further aft, intent on lobbing something through a port. Two men behind them died instantly when a light machine-gun appeared and loosed off a short burst.

Nick's nerves were beginning to jump in case the same thing happened again, but young Billy Thomas was the hero of that minute. He rose on his knees, and actually tossed a grenade through one of the after ports with no more concern than if he had been enjoying himself on a fairground.

Horsfall put in another from closer, and Nick fired a Sten in short bursts through the ports. A little later, heavier fire from B troop's perimeter against the port side made them retire directly behind the tail. The resistance, which had been spirited, folded.

The Major and his captains appeared to be on the spot in no time. Runners were up with them from various points on the extremities. Between them, the three senior officers sorted out the gist of the information.

'It appears that three glider loads of the Boches are creeping up on us, lads. You recollect what I was saying before these blighters broke up our briefing. I want you sappers, if you still have heart for the job, to work your way round the various gullies and crevasses which lead up to our position and put every kind of device that you can think of to stop the enemy from crawling in on us. After all, the weather's bad enough without having to share billets with the Hun!'

Dunstable looked fit and well, having recovered from his earlier arm wound. His sally drew a grin from men who had been fighting hard only a minute or two earlier.

A Troop's sappers had lost five men, but that long Welsh sapling of a Rugby Union wing three-quarter who commanded them, 'Dai' Jimmy Jones, was not at all daunted. He, it was, with a solemn furrowing of the brow, who asked the important question.

'Tell me, sir, which side is most likely to be threatened by the glider troops while we're sealing off the gullies?'

Dunstable nodded. 'A good question, Jones. The runners tell me we're likely to have twice as many of the Boche on the south-east side as on the north-west.'

Jones cleared his throat to speak, but Nick Burrows beat him to it. He also managed to make his voice and utterance matter of fact.

'With respect, sir, I'd like to point out that Section One of Troop B only lost two, except for the death of our officer. As we have such numerical superiority, I think we should tackle the south-east perimeter.'

'Those are my thoughts on the matter exactly,' Dunstable returned smoothly.

Nick straightened up, and sensed that his section had done the same behind him. 'Then with your permission, sir, we'll collect our gear and make a start. I intend to work from the quiet end towards the trouble. I think it very unlikely that the Germans will expect to find any of us over the edge.'

Nick waited a moment while the Major conferred quietly with Captain Burns. Burns it was who turned to them. 'Don't be afraid to get in touch with our boys directly above you if you want anything. We'll send messengers round to tell the men to keep a very special lookout for you. We're sorry about Lieutenant Maine, but we were most impressed by the way you tackled the glider. Well done, and good luck.'

The new corporal expressed his thanks, wished the other section the best of luck and raced his men to the stores. There, they collected a fair amount of barbed wire, and the apparatus of booby traps and small mines.

Five minutes later, they were over the rim at a quiet point on A Troop's sector, south-east side. They worked their way towards the north-east very slowly and with much caution. The man lowest on the slope was furthest forward. The man above him was a couple of yards behind, and so on in that formation until Nick, the top man, who was furthest back.

All the time, they kept in close touch, watching what was going on above them, and studying the places from which the enemy fired back. There were three gullies worthy of mention along that slope. The first two were filled with concertina wire and a few booby traps. The job was done in a very economic time and with no incidents. The third gully, about a hundred yards away from the nearest known Germans, also looked as if it would not give much trouble. The paratroops on the saddle rim above had worked hard to clear the slope near the gully, knowing that the sappers would be in danger if they failed.

Working from the top, Nick spilled out the wire and passed it on from man to man down the line. There was some rooting in the soil, and shifting of small rocks and stones before the wire was placed to everyone's satisfaction.

The end of the wire actually ran out about five yards above a sharp narrowing of the gully. Jake Shaw, the lowest operating sapper, was conveying this information back to the top by mime when a sizeable rock, loosened very largely by the rains, slipped from its regular place and crashed on the former policeman's leg. He gave a sharp cry of pain, and found difficulty in turning at all because the leg was trapped.

This emergency had Nick baffled for a minute or two. Finally, he decided to step clear of the cleft and get down the sheltered side of it as fast as he could. Just as he was about to set off, a Schmeisser sounded off from within ten to fifteen yards of poor Shaw's pinned body. The two men directly below Nick cried out and crumpled.

'Krauts down 'ere, Corp!' Shaw yelled, biting back pain. 'A grenade is what's wanted!'

'Hold on,' Nick yelled back, his mouth drying out. While he hesitated, he saw the top of the nearest German's helmet. It was much closer to Shaw than he had thought. He could not hurl a grenade in case he killed his own man. His voice was hoarse when he ordered two men to assist the wounded up to the saddle, and the rest to give him covering fire, if it was needed. He licked his lips, took a firm grip of his Sten and actually rolled down the slope. It was a wild thing to do. Any small rock jarring his hands might have started the light machine-gun off.

By luck rather than skill, he stopped about five yards below the trapped sapper. As soon as he was prone, he eliminated the nearest German with a lucky ricochet. A grenade took care of the other two who were close while they were trying to think how the Corporal should be dealt with.

Nick had to lie down on his back and press both his bent legs against the pinioning rock before it rolled clear and careered on down the slope. Shaw's leg was badly hurt, but he managed a grin, nevertheless.

'Thanks for that sterling effort,' he remarked, between sudden bouts of pain. 'Here.'

He fumbled inside his tunic and pulled out a miniature sized bottle of whisky. A mere tiny thing which he had been carrying about with him ever since he left home. Wounded man and corporal shared it, rolling it round their mouths and tongues.

Nick got down on his knees and picked Shaw up. He had to go over his shoulder in a fireman's lift. 'Now don't you go bothering your head if I start whimpering or anything,' Shaw advised.

'Okay, Jake. Nothing guaranteed this trip, mind.'

The young man started up the

punishing slope with his burden. All around them, so it seemed, bullets were flying and the war was going on apace. Nick remembered passing the first two men who were standing by to give him covering fire if necessary. All that interminable time, perhaps two minutes in all, Shaw's body was rigid with pain. Quite unaccountably, shortly after that, he suddenly relaxed. Even so, some fifty yards further on, Nick's legs gave out, and Horsfall and Thomas put up their weapons and came to his aid unbidden. They took the head between them and backed up the slope, while Nick retained the legs, one sound and the other twisted and crushed.

A minute elapsed before he realized the truth. Shaw's trunk had absorbed a stray bullet while on his back. He was dead.

Nick's grimy face was streaked with tears as he staggered over the rim and firm hands came out on all sides to assist.

14

Four hours after the fighting started, the last of the enemy automatic fire faded and died. Dunstable waited until dusk before putting out two small recce patrols to make sure whether the approach slopes were really cleared of the enemy, or whether some sort of stratagem was being employed for a further attack by stealth.

The patrols were away for a little over an hour. When they returned it was quite clear that the glider-borne assault had failed and that no one had survived, unless they had retreated down into the valley.

The field ambulance unit was very busy that night. Upwards of a score of men had been killed in repulsing the glider troops and the shrinking of overall numbers was something which the paras could scarcely afford. The struggle with the Germans, the Italians and the weather looked as though it was going to be long and bitter.

There was still activity back in Algiers, but relief troops were slow in getting through the hills to the scene of the fighting. Volunteers dug the graves of the deceased, and the padre gave a solemn burial service for them by the light of a moon frequently hidden by scudding cloud.

Many men attended the service and Nick found himself side by side with Sergeant Johnson, Wright, Pawson, Potts and Smith. He was glad to rub shoulders with them at a time when he was only just realizing that his section had suffered as much in the gully work as the other sappers had done when the glider dropped in on them.

A Troop sappers were reduced to one subaltern and seven men. B Troop, one corporal and seven. Together, they were the total strength of engineers in the whole party, but then there was little of an engineering nature left for such men to do. Their greatest use to their country at that time was to fight hard and help hold the ground.

That very same week, the Germans under Marshal Rommel and General Von Arnim made a strong armoured push against the central positions of the Allies a little further south than the sector held by the British. Tanks, advancing in depth, caught the lesser experienced United States 2nd Corps unprepared. Insufficient tanks were massed and manœuvred by the Americans and consequently, the German advance could not be halted.

Rommel, if he was on the spot, began to roll everything before him. The Allied High Command began to get really worried about this thrust. The British First Army was drawn into the struggle. With very little warning, the artillery and armour on which the paras had been able to call at times for support was suddenly whipped away further south to help arrest the German advance.

The paratroops felt naked and very vulnerable on their hill saddle, knowing that they would have to fend entirely for themselves in the event of a concerted attack on their position. The first day was one of considerably anxiety. The hills were shrouded in mist, and visibility was bad.

The sky was clear of the enemy for that day, and no troops attempted to win the slopes which the glider troops had failed to capture earlier. But the respite, with the artillery and armour withdrawn, simply could not go on for long. After one day of suspense, long range German artillery began to pump shells into the saddle. First they dropped down the rear slope, up which the troop carriers had first come. Then they improved range and started to burst just below the rim of the saddle on that side.

Every shell made a crater, and a man was lucky on the north-west flank if his slit trench remained intact while the small blasted rocks and stones were flying about. Major Dunstable became anxious. It was not clear to him what this softening up process was leading to. From his tiny H.Q. unit he sent picked men around the perimeter to confer with the best lookouts. Nothing new was learned.

While the mist persisted, a recce patrol went over the rim with orders not to go below thirty yards from the saddle. They started out on the south-east side of the great bulking pinnacle and worked their way in a clockwise direction round the whole fortification without apprehending any skulking German troops, or learning anything new.

They were soaking wet, breathless and red-faced when they were assisted into the defensive ring from the north-east side of the pinnacle. Only the great bulking finger of rock had prevented them from making a complete circle.

The subaltern in charge relayed his information to Dunstable and the captains during a lull in the artillery barrage. While they were conferring, other men were hurriedly digging out about a dozen paras who had been half buried when their trenches were blasted in.

'So we're right back where we started from,' Dunstable remarked grimly. 'No trace of an assault anywhere. It doesn't seem natural to me, heaving all those shells at us if we aren't to be attacked.'

He glanced round the tent, which he was using as his headquarters, and saw only confirmation of his own thoughts in the faces of officers and men with him. Minutes later, he stood up and was about to dismiss the assembled gathering when a sound which was quite familiar disturbed them.

Dunstable grabbed his tin hat and raced out of doors followed by the others. They searched the sky, or what they could see of it. The sound was that of aircraft engines; probably those of a Stuka. It appeared to be moving up on them from the other side of the pinnacle. They strained their eyes, and some used glasses but the plane remained hidden to them. As the upper part of the pinnacle was ringed in mist, perhaps this was to be expected.

As near as the men could judge, the top of the pinnacle was about seven hundred feet above their saddle. They remembered this as the Stuka's engines were heard directly over the top of the landmark. It had been approaching for anything up to half a minute since they first heard it. Now, it seemed to be too close to go into a dive aimed at the saddle.

There were other modes of attack, however; perhaps the aim was to drop bombs from a relatively high altitude. Every man stood alerted. Suddenly the fighter-bomber popped out of the mist cap and droned across their bit of sky. A couple of Brens greeted it and then gave up, so as not to waste ammunition.

The pilot flew on and passed out of sight again, and that seemed to be the end of the incident until another Stuka did exactly the same. The second one flew over the paras' positions at an even higher altitude and disappeared from view rather quicker. The men on the ground were baffled. They remained in that state until something they were very familiar with swam through the upper atmosphere towards them. It was a grey parachute with a canister dangling from the harness.

So that was it! Airborne supplies, but for an enemy they had failed to locate. The mystery had now gathered more substance. There was a good deal of hard thinking going on as the parachute landed in the paras' area and Lieutenant 'Dai' Jones went forward to open it in case it was booby trapped.

It was found that the canister was perfectly innocent. All it contained was action food rations for troops. It was a little bit off course, that was all. The lookouts were doubled, but no attempt was made to send out another patrol.

The sapper subaltern was in a good mood, having distinguished himself over the canister. He beamed as Nick Burrows approached him, and offered a rather dubious German forces issue cigarette. Nick took one. He struck a match for the two of them, and when his cigarette was going, he broached the matter uppermost in his mind.

'Sir, you're the only sapper officer up here now, I wondered if you'd have any objection if I approached the C.O. with a suggestion?'

'Sure you don't want to tell me about it first, Burrows?'

Jones looked rather crestfallen, but he recovered quite quickly. Nick had shrugged and looked mildly embarrassed, and the subaltern was quick to curtail the awkward moment. 'Please go ahead.

Don't upset your Troop Commander or anything, though, will you?'

Nick nodded, thanked him and saluted for good measure. He trotted across the great saucer-like depression, pulling up until three shells had sailed over the position, and then going on as before. He found Captain Burns and the C.O. hunched over a map of the area looking baffled.

The sergeant-major looked at the C.O. for guidance as Nick appeared in the doorway. Dunstable waved him in, and looked keenly into his face. 'You look like a fellow who's just had a bright idea, Burrows. Let's hear about it!'

Nick made his salute and relaxed. 'Sir, I've been thinking. If tunnels can be ruled out, it has to be the pinnacle.'

Burns looked baffled. He waited for Dunstable to comment on the curt suggestion. The C.O. made an open-handed gesture towards Nick, and the sergeant-major moved closer to listen. The intentness of his audience made Nick stammer for a moment, but he recovered.

'Dropped supplies suggest the enemy's

in the area. Probably thinking of having a go at us after the bombardment lets up. If they are anywhere above the valley floor it must be directly behind the pinnacle, sir. That big steeple of rock is our blind spot. I have a feeling there's a gully runs right up to the foot of the pinnacle. Men and materials could be smuggled up it, and in ordinary circumstances we shouldn't know about them until it was too late.'

Burns gasped. The sergeant-major cleared his throat. Dunstable nodded unhappily. 'What then do you suppose is the enemy's plan, Burrows?'

'I don't rightly know, sir. What they *ought* to be doing, though, is manhandling some of their light field guns up to that collar round the pinnacle so that they can put down some steady fire right into our midst!'

The red-faced sergeant-major headed for the tent flap. 'The collar is just hidden in the mist at the moment, sir,' Nick added. 'The only alternative to sending out more patrols is to let a few good climbers go up our face of the pinnacle and see for themselves what's happenin'' over the other side. If I'm wrong, we could still locate a couple of guns up there, and if I'm right, we could blast the Germans right back where they started from, guns an' all!'

'Do you really think they could get light field guns up to that collar, Burrows?'

'Why not, sir? After all, the gradient on the other side of the pinnacle is much easier than our side.'

'Do you think they may be climbing now?'

'It's possible, sir, but I'd say they won't get themselves properly organized until the mist lifts. Perhaps tomorrow.'

'When were you thinking of starting the climb Burrows?' Dunstable asked.

A few seconds later, a bewildered expression crossed his face as he realized that he had anticipated what he thought the N.C.O. was going to say. Before he could apologize, Nick was quick to answer.

'Why, as soon as the mist will allow, sir!'

Burns grinned. Dunstable joined in, and the sergeant-major pretended he had been out of earshot all the time. The latter had a long rubbery mobile face, a long nose and a short Kraut-style haircut. His put-on innocent expression would not have fooled the rawest recruit.

Late in the afternoon, the artillery stopped and did not start again. The intermittent rain also stopped about six in the evening. The paras watched the mist round the pinnacle like a bunch of weather experts, but it made no attempt to remove itself. It was still there when those who could turned in for the night.

A surprisingly large number of men awakened early the following morning. They lay in the bottom of their trenches smoking their early morning cigarettes and wondering when the Royal Air Force was going to take a leaf out of the *Luftwaffe*'s book and drop them the overdue supplies.

Their eyes were drawn to the pinnacle and the small mist cloud which was slowly dispersing at six hundred feet up. The collar was clearly in view. It did not go all the way round the neck of the pinnacle. On the saddle side it was non-existent, and on the far side, where the infiltration was likely to be, a fringe of old talus rocks made movement around the collar difficult.

Nick Burrows, Red Horsfall and Billy Thomas ate the best breakfast the cooks could provide. It looked like being an all sapper effort. Lieutenant Jones and the rest of the men of the two sapper sections had charge of the ground work at the foot of the climb. Those who were not going aloft, looked with envy at the corporal and his two assistants.

Although all sections had been given a chance to provide volunteers for the climb, Thomas and Horsfall had won the right to be roped to their N.C.O. In Thomas' case, this was not surprising. He lived in the Llanberis area, and had experience of mountain rescue. Horsfall got the other place by sheer persistence. He was an expert potholer, but what finally tipped the balance in his favour was his ability to flash morse at fifteen words a minute, self taught.

Between them, Nick and his assistants took up with them a Bren, a few grenades and explosives, and a strong manilla rope and pulley which would be useful for hauling up anything else of a vital nature. Upwards of a score of men stood at the foot of the pinnacle, watching the climb start, and prominent among them were Sergeant Johnson and the other old friends who had shared earlier adventures.

Nick moved up steadily, encouraging Thomas and Horsfall by his example. The lookouts were enjoined to do a good job, in case the climbers were exposed to the enemy at a critical time. Once or twice the feet of the climbers loosened stones and soil, but nothing untoward happened as they worked their way higher.

The four hundred feet to the collar seemed much higher than it really was, and only the last fifty feet were really difficult. The last hazard took the form of a chimney, but Nick tackled it with a rope and grappling hook. As soon as he had hauled himself clear onto the wind swept and wet surface of the collar, he did a short recce.

There were man-made sounds which

indicated that his earlier speculation was right, but the enemy remained out of sight beyond the talus. He turned and gave his attention to the determined pair tackling the chimney. As soon as Horsfall had got his breath back, he flashed a message saying that all was well so far, and that man-made noises were coming from the other side.

Dunstable had an acknowledgement flashed back and counselled them to be cautious. Nick signalled with his red beret, and promptly set off along the collar. The damp wind sought to chill them to the marrow, but they felt exhilarated because of their achievement.

Soon, they were moving with great caution across the top of the talus. Yard by yard they edged round the age-old heap towards the sound of the noises. A man who looked like an Austrian mountain guide was leaning over the edge and looking directly down the side of the pinnacle hidden from the saddle. A rope was creaking through a pulley beside him, and obviously some heavy weight was being drawn up.

Nick pointed to the man and touched his finger to his lips. He moved a little closer, bringing his Sten up under his right arm. A sudden premonition made the man look round. He was wholly baffled when he saw Nick sitting on top of the talus with the wind tearing at him. The soldier, one of a crack Austrian mountain regiment, turned, ducked and made a grab for his automatic weapon.

A spiked boot slipped on a wet rock and down he went, under the sharp burst which Nick fired at him. He rolled away from the source of human danger, hovered unbelievingly on the brink beside the pulley apparatus and suddenly fell out of sight. His scarcely human cry shook all three British climbers to the core.

Several minutes elapsed before Nick could bring himself to look down beyond the pulley. It was clear enough what was happening. Some two hundred feet lower down, where the precipitate slope eased out a little, were upwards of a score of mountain troopers who had been hauling on a rope to lift a light field gun. The gun in question, which was the first of several, hung about seventy feet below Nick's position, just wide of the talus.

Obviously the men below thought their comrade had simply slipped. They had no idea that he had encountered the enemy. Nick saw them without being seen. With the Bren, he could have blasted through the manilla rope and dropped the field gun on the toilers below, but somehow that did not seem fair. They had to be eliminated. It was them or the British paras. But a few unexpected bullets were better than a crashing gun.

Horsfall had the Bren. He brought it along without any prompting and aimed it at the group lower down. At a nod from Nick, he squeezed the trigger. The Austrians began to fall about in all directions, seemingly in slow motion. From above they had no protection. Red did not stop until they were all knocked out, and the field gun was swinging above them like a pendulum.

It was not hard to lever the rock which had held the pulley secure over the parapet. Down went the gun. It fell like a toy, and bounced quite high before it plunged like scrap iron past the next three guns assembled below.

Automatic weapons fired back at the collar, although nothing much could be known about the strength of the paras. A tall officer started to harangue his men and drive them up the cleft which had proved so useful. Obviously, they were going to take a lot more dissuading than Nick had thought. He took over the Bren himself and sent the other two back to the saddle side of the pinnacle. There, they were to request that a mortar be sent up, along with a useful number of bombs.

Meanwhile, Nick studied the rock surface near where the enemy outfit had had the pulley. With a piece of chalk, he marked several places where he wanted to use demolition charges. They had to be chosen carefully so as not to risk a landslide.

The mortar appeared in quicker time than he had expected. They rigged it up and aimed the sensitively-fused bombs at the poor Austrians who had been exhorted to attack up the narrow cleft. None of the paras were experts with the mortar, but soon they had the range and the accuracy. Every other bomb wounded or killed men, and some of those which went wide added to the general confusion by blasting in the sides of the approach cleft.

When all the bombs were used up, the gully was full of still forms. It had been a massacre of sorts. An attack from the unexpected angle. While the mortar was going down again, Nick set his charges with twenty minute fuses. As soon as this was done, he went back to the chimney and indicated that he wanted to start the descent.

The descent began, and the worst of it was over when the charges started to go up. All the paras could see was the occasional fall of small debris, but the sounds carried to them and shook the hills around.

Nick moved into the presence of his waiting comrades fully confident that no other mountain troops would be in a hurry to attempt a climb on the pinnacle.

In fact, after they saw what had happened to the Austrians, they could be forgiven for having second thoughts.

The trio received a full-throated cheer as they slipped out of the harness of rope which had held them together for the descent. Their ears were still buzzing with the noise and their shoulders ached with being slapped when they entered the C.O.'s tent and gave him a full account of what they had done.

Dunstable checked the facts, shook hands with them and led them out of the tent. Outside, they found the remaining sappers under Lieutenant Jones drawn up as for a parade. To his surprise, Nick became the centre of attraction. In a loud, clear voice, Dunstable told of his latest exploit from first to last. He ended with his own personal congratulations, and finally pinned another stripe beneath the two which already decorated his uniform tunic.

For a few seconds, Nick wished his brother, Harry, was there and then he was back among his comrades, blushing for all he was worth and living the moment as though it was his last.

He walked away stunned with joy, and wondered if this meant he ought to sign on as a long serviceman when the war was over.

15

In the thrust against the American front, Rommel kept going until finally he over-extended himself. He had turned north towards the British positions, and that turn enabled the American armour to catch up with him. A series of hard blows on his flank opened up a threat to his infantry and armour, and to prevent his losing the initiative, he went back on his tracks for the best part of fifty miles.

His sortie in force, although he had finally been contained, had won a lot of time. Furthermore, he had captured a good deal of useful material abandoned by the Americans in their flight. Tanks, and vehicles, for instance, which had been slightly damaged came in very useful for the combined German armies in Tunisia.

The Afrika Korps' commander then planned a big tank thrust against his old antagonist, the Eighth Army. This attack was thwarted due to a simple, but very effective trick. The forward anti-tank gun pits were really dummies, and when the Desert Rats abandoned them, apparently in a panic, the dusty armour surged forward to be hit without warning by six-pounder armour-piercing shells. The guns were more than a match for the iron-clads, and when he withdrew, the Desert Fox had lost about fifty which were promptly destroyed.

Rommel continued to be in contact with the Eighth Army while other forces struggled elsewhere.

★ ★ ★

Although the paratroops' saddle in the British sector of the hills had proved more or less impregnable, the dwindling force of Red Devils were suffering in other respects. Their supplies were pitifully low, and as no road transport could get to them, they were dependent upon drops from the air. Several drops had gone astray. At first, the loss of the parachute supplies was thought to be accidental, but soon they realized that the enemy was interfering with the stores planes.

No less than three times in six days the parachutes drifted across the valley towards hills occupied by the enemy. Each time, enemy anti-aircraft fire was responsible, and it became more and more effective. On the first occasion, a patrol was sent out of the saddle at dusk. All night long, the hungry men waited for news of them but they never returned. It was supposed that some of the not infrequent sharp bursts of automatic gunfire heard in the night had accounted for them.

At the second setback, the Germans were actually seen collecting the canisters the following dawn. When the enemy availed themselves of the food for a second time in this way, the paras were too dispirited and lacking in stamina to be properly angry.

The Allied High Command had tried to relieve the Red Devils on two occasions, but each time the relieving troops had had to be switched to another part of the front. The paras lost confidence in the remote planners in

Algiers, and Dunstable, who had acquired a few more grey hairs, expressed himself open to suggestions.

He heard no less than five from men who had never been capable of constructive thought before, but their suggestions were hopeless.

Nick Burrows' brain remained dormant until the day when he started to experience mild rheumatic pains in his back. The twinges stimulated his thoughts. The food was not getting through; neither were the relieving troops. The winter was slowly passing, but hard-pressed men could not live that out in conditions of great privation without sustenance. To make the situation worse, the ammunition position was not much better than that of the food.

Nick had taken to mingling with his older comrades in a canvas-covered dugout during lulls in the evenings. Red Horsfall and Billy Thomas, who had achieved sudden notoriety due to their climb up the pinnacle, were always welcome in the company of Scouse Johnson, and the others.

Sergeant Johnson and Corporal Wright were both delighted to see the sapper trio on the evening when Nick's brain started to calculate. It was quite an event for the older comrades because Scouse was weakened since a piece of shrapnel lodged in his leg, and Lofty had a troublesome wound in his shoulder.

When they were all seated in the bottom of the dugout, Johnson yawned and asked Nick for his view of things. The newly promoted sergeant was slow to answer. 'We need another drop, a special one,' he suggested at last. 'Plenty of grub in it, and a few choice items of ammunition. A kind of Malta convoy that has to get through, see? Only this time, we have to be out of here and ready in the place where the stuff is likely to drop.'

'According to what I could find out, the wind's in the same direction as it was when the other canisters dropped wide,' Jock Pawson suggested. 'If I've understood you, that means the collectors would have to be under it across the valley there, right under the Jerry-held hills.'

'That's what I meant, Jock. It will mean a small force climbing out of here the night before, and the canisters being dropped deliberately where they fell before. I think that could be arranged. As far as the collectors are concerned, it would be a do or die effort. They couldn't take much ammo with them because we're short. The same with food. They'd have to rely on what was in the canisters, and if the Boche beat them to it, it would mean a quick death, or captivity.'

There was a grim note of finality in his voice as he made this last statement. He glanced round the ring of straggly beards and wondered if they felt and looked as scruffy as he did. His own luxuriant growth of blue-black beard was over an inch long.

'How would it be if we got there ahead of the Germans?' Ginger Potts queried.

'Well, we could take out the stores and booby trap the containers,' Nick explained. 'And given the chances, we might be able to smuggle some of the stores back up here. I think it might be worth a try, provided we don't get relief in the ordinary way.'

'How many men do you reckon ought to go, Nick?' Pongo Smith asked quietly.

'About half a dozen, I'd say. If nothing much happens tomorrow, I'll try and get the C.O. interested. It would be a big step to take, but I think the time is not far off when we might have to take it.'

The listeners looked at one another very thoughtfully. Obviously the two wounded would not be able to go. The sortie would mean a parting, and perhaps a permanent one.

* * *

Nothing happened to improve the situation the following day.

It was almost thirty hours exactly from the time when Nick's plan was first discussed when the selected party went over the rim of the defensive saddle and started down the slope. The time was four a.m. and it was hoped that they would have crossed the valley floor before dawn light began to probe the lower altitudes.

Major Dunstable had at once taken to

the plan to try and safeguard the dropped supplies. He had wirelessed back to base a specially coded message requesting the drop on a certain day at a certain time, and suggested that if the canisters fell wide it would not be a very serious setback. It was hinted that a party would be out of the hills and waiting by the spot where earlier drops had gone astray.

Finally, it was suggested that the same pilot and aircrew be used, and the same approach route, too.

High Command took an hour or so to peruse and think over the message, and finally came through with full approval. Sergeant Burrows was called into the presence and formally asked if it was his intention to go with the stores party and command it. He assured his officers that it was, and that he wanted to pick his own men from the volunteers who hoped to go with him. This concession was granted, and his advice was taken as to numbers, and what they could take with them.

Nick chose as his companions a mixture of old and new comrades. The old squad were presented by Jock

Pawson, Ginger Potts and Pongo Smith, while Billy Thomas and Red Horsfall came from the new. The leave taking with Scouse Johnson and Lofty Wright, and other close friends, took a long time on that last night.

Many men left their sleeping bags especially to come and shake hands with the determined half dozen who might not get back. So touching was the parting that every man who was leaving had the firm impression that he was not expected back. Within five minutes they were out of sight from the saddle and making good progress down a slope which was beginning to show signs that spring was approaching.

They climbed down in a short snake column with Nick in the lead, Pongo, Ginger and Pawson following up close, and Horsfall and Thomas, the two young sappers, bringing up the rear. On the downgrade, they were almost scrambling into one another because of initial anxiety and a desire to make progress while the going was easy.

After half an hour, Potts missed his

footing and sprawled on his face, banging his nose on a flat rock. The blood started to spurt from it. The others suddenly stood motionless, and then went to his aid. A brief scrambling noise less than twenty yards away made their hearts palpitate.

Potts quickly recovered his poise. They moved towards the source of the sound very stealthily, and to their relief they found a hardy mountain sheep caught in a thicket. Pongo slit its throat and there was some discussion as to whether they could take it with them.

'We haven't got the time to cut it up, or to carry it, lads,' Nick pointed out. 'If we *do* get back this way, it might come in very useful, though. All we can do is mark the spot and hope for the best.'

So guided, Pongo drove a tree branch into the ground and stuck his red beret on the top of it. He made sure it would not blow away and hurriedly joined the rest. After that, their rate of progress was a little slower. Around five o'clock, when the upper reaches of the hills were experiencing the light of a new day, they started to ghost across the valley floor. It was rough and uneven, but their ankles and legs were in no special danger, provided they kept a sharp lookout for boulders. Twenty minutes later, they had made the crossing and were moving up into the nearest slope towards the south-east.

Nick kept them climbing for perhaps five hundred feet. At that particular height there were several dark openings in the rock face. The third one which they examined appeared to be the mouth of a cave. At once, their spirits rose. They moved inside, explored its depths and began to divest themselves of their Everests. Soon, they had lined up in the opening and were watching the bright light of day creep down the opposite slope at the top of which were their comrades.

The signs augured fine weather. Their early breakfast had not worked its way through them, and soon they were ready for sleep. A small fire helped to take the dampness out of the atmosphere at the back of the cave. They had the smoke to contend with, but that did not seem to trouble them. Every man slept until mid-afternoon.

★   ★   ★

The Allied supply planes came at the appointed time. They were Dakotas, two in number. At a certain distance from the dropping zone the Germans started to put up their concentrated anti-aircraft fire. 88mm. guns and others of different calibre filled the sky with dark grey puffs a half hour before dusk.

Nick's party waited with bated breath while each plane struggled through the hostile flak and disgorged its supplies. Three parachutes opened behind each plane and soon the six canisters were well on their way down. One plane's 'chutes appeared to have been dropped fairly accurately. The first parachute dipped out of sight beyond the saddle. The second actually fell within the defensive ring, and the third draped itself about a third of the way down the slope which the stores party had negotiated. That third canister was perhaps fifty yards away from the slaughtered sheep. The watchers hoped that if it was recovered the dead animal would also be seen and taken away for food.

Nick thought the canister would be recovered with the grappling hook on the end of a rope. If that were so, then the sheep would probably remain unnoticed.

The ack-ack fire faded and stopped as the peppered supply planes pulled out and headed towards the west. Meanwhile, the second trio of three canisters swung easily under their canopies and neared terra firma. These might have been laid on specially for the foraging party. Two dropped in the middle of the valley floor, perhaps fifty yards to westward of the vehicle track. And the third one clattered gently down at the foot of the slope where they had established themselves.

'When do we start, Nick?' Ginger asked.

During the spell on the saddle he had taken to biting his nails, and now they were very short. Billy Thomas shifted his feet uneasily, and Jock Pawson showed by his gaze that his thoughts were back in the saddle with Lofty. Horsfall and Smith remained quite calm. They had a similar outlook although Smith was a year or two older and a regular soldier.

'As soon as the darkness gets low enough to hide us,' Nick decided. 'I've got a feeling there are more Germans in this area than we know about. That being so, I want to rig up a few surprises for them. Jock, I'd like you an' Ginger and Pongo to start unloading that nearest canister as soon as we get down there. Shift the contents to one side, at least twenty yards away an' don't make 'em look too obvious. Right?'

Jock nodded, and the two young sappers waited for their instructions.

Nick went on. 'I want you two to rig up a necklace of mines just above the location of the canister for the benefit of any Germans who scramble down the slope towards it. Me, I shall put a device or two actually in or near the canister just to make sure we don't waste our time.'

'How about the other two canisters? We shall have to crawl after them, won't we?' Pawson queried.

'Perhaps so,' Nick concurred. 'But we'll see about them when this other little surprise party is worked out. Everybody ready to go?'

There was a chorus of agreement. One after another they left the cave which had sheltered them.

★   ★   ★

In spite of the coolness of the evening, they started to perspire as soon as they reached the canister and started working on their allotted assignments. The canister contained a Bren gun, a lot of spare ammunition and various kinds of preserved foods. Pawson, Potts and Smith worked to empty it and to take away the contents as Nick had suggested. In the daylight, it would have taken very little time, but darkness prolonged the task and made them breathless.

Red Horsfall and Billy Thomas moved back up the slope a few yards and rigged the necklace of mines which was meant to impede Germans coming down the slope. To them it seemed rather ridiculous to expect the enemy to be using the same slope as they had negotiated earlier, but as Red pointed out, Jerry had to come from somewhere. It was either down the slope or along the valley floor. Nick fixed his little anti-personnel devices with the thoroughness which had always been characteristic of his technical work. He was busily checking over the fitting of the second when a foreign sound impinged upon his eardrums.

Horsfall rasped his forefinger against his thumb rather rapidly, producing a sound like a low-pitched grasshopper noise. This was the warning signal, and it meant that they had to be prepared for uninvited guests.

Nick satisfied himself about his handiwork. At the foot of that slope it was impossible to see more than a yard or two. He glanced round in the direction of the other three. He sensed that they were standing beside the heap of stores, awaiting the word to start transferring it elsewhere.

Red murmured: 'Krauts above us, coming down. Anything from four to six.

Not much time.'

'You two leave that necklace. Move out slowly and carefully, one to one side, the other to the other. Wide of the ends, understand? Get well away and keep quiet.'

A couple of grunts assured him that they understood. Nick snapped his fingers for the benefit of Pawson and company. He received the same signal back. At once, he started to wriggle backwards, away from the canister and towards the pile of stores. The sounds of heavy boots half stumbling down the slope grew louder. The Germans did not expect to contact anyone from the saddle. According to their calculations there had not been time since the drop for *Englanders* to reach the valley.

Every British ear strained to pick out the number of voices. Some thought three. One thought five, and most would have settled for four. Suddenly a heavily-built man stumbled over the wire. Three or four Teutonic oaths were on the point of being uttered as two others sprawled over him.

Abruptly the mines went up. First one, in a sheet of reddish orange flame, and then two more in quick succession. In the almost blinding flash the watchers saw four bodies sprawl in all directions, probably already dead before they hit the ground. Nick put in a fast panned burst with his Sten to account for two more, and then he desisted.

The echoes of the explosions plumbed the depths of the valley and kept the senses away from the smell of scorched earth and flesh. The work of the two young sappers had been diabolically successful, but fears were building up in the minds of the British trio furthest away from the scene of the destruction.

Ginger Potts' anxious voice said: 'Nick! Are you all right? Will you show yourself, or something?'

'Just a cough would do,' Jock Pawson added hastily.

No more than three seconds later, two powerful automatic weapons from different points on the valley floor opened up on the place where the shouts came from. Back and forth the weapons were panned, first at chest height and then lower. Nick dropped his head on his crooked arm. A soundless cry of horror came from his open mouth. Jock, Ginger and Pongo . . . Could any of them have lived through those Spandau bursts? *Could they? Or had they died because of their concern for his safety?*

Horsfall and Thomas remained silent. They must have realized what had happened. Nick waited for five minutes after the bursts of fire had finished. He then started to crawl towards the place where the mines had gone off. Thomas was at his elbow in no time, and Horsfall took about three minutes to rejoin them.

Nick groaned. 'Those were good fighting men and good friends, lads. Don't endanger your own lives by calling out to find out about another.' His voice shook as he gave them this advice.

He took them back to the heap of the stores where Pawson, Smith and Potts had been cut down. All three of them had died instantly under the withering fire. Thomas and Horsfall would have stayed to bury them, if he had said the word, but he knew that they could not afford to take any more risks with untold numbers of Germans loose along the valley floor. Between them, they scrambled some soil and rocks over the dead men. Their faces were covered with their helmets and their weapons laid beside them. Nick helped himself to one or two photographs and letters and then he stood up.

'One of you grab that Bren and the other some ammo. Also we require as much of the food as we can manage for one trip. We may not get down this way again.'

'Back to the cave, is it?' the Welshman asked.

Nick nodded, and Red shouldered the Bren.

16

At the cave they relit the fire which was well back and laid out their spoils by the light it gave. They kept off talking about the men who had died down below, but Nick's thoughts kept slipping back to them; particularly to Ginger Potts who had once hated him because of the death of his officer, Lieutenant Casson. Ginger had blamed him for quite a long time, and now he had died because he was over-anxious about Nick's fate.

Ginger's need to look up to somebody with loyalty and affection had brought about his downfall. Nick thought his end was tragic.

They made themselves a good meal out of tinned bacon and other things and ate until their stomachs were almost distended. At the beginning of the meal, Nick made certain things clear.

'We were very lucky to get across here without being seen, and a return journey would obviously be much more perilous. I'm of the opinion that we should strike towards the east or the south, do what damage we can and seek to join up with other Allied units. There are bound to be some about. Yanks or Frenchmen, or what have you. How do you two feel about moving on instead of going back?'

Neither of the others agreed blindly. They thought it out and discussed it for another five minutes before falling in with Nick's suggestion. He started to feel calmer when he had their agreement. Once again he set his watch for an early hour in the morning. Shortly before four a.m. he awakened the other two and prepared a brew of tea. While they drank theirs, he stood in the entrance to the cave and smoked a cigarette, of which they had plenty.

'Grab what you can standing up, lads, because in a few minutes we're going out, up and round, and we shan't be coming back this way.'

They shared a tin of beans and some biscuits before repacking their knapsacks and expressing themselves ready to move.

Nick nodded, looked them over and led the way. For a while, he was content to make his way with safety at the same level towards the east, then, as their muscles started to respond better and a faint greyness crept into the upper atmosphere he aimed for greater altitude.

As he climbed he thought how useful that climb up the pinnacle had been in showing him the calibre of these two young sappers. He began to wonder how far they would get, and how long they would remain together.

The false dawn was giving way to the real one when he found the shallow niche on the hillside. He drew them into it after him and lit three cigarettes. For the first time since the climb started, he permitted them to look down into the valley which they had negotiated earlier. The mist was slow to disperse down there, but the binoculars were still useful.

Nick had just spotted the place where they had left the canister when they became aware of about twelve men in field grey creeping cautiously towards it with their weapons to hand. Four went ahead of the rest to inspect it, and finally two of them — having decided it was intact — moved to grip the canister at the ends.

Simultaneously, Nick's anti-personnel devices exploded. The container was lifted and the unfortunate pair blown backwards. Another man was near enough to be seriously injured. The sapper sergeant was apparently acting out of character when he stood up and laughed at their fate.

He stooped and spat into the valley, and staring across towards the distant pinnacle, he murmured: 'That's for Jock, and Ginger an' Pongo. Amen.'

On they went again, this time with no backward looks. They crossed a ridge late in the day, one which Nick felt sure was between German-held hills and Allied territory, but the Allies were nowhere to be found. During the prolonged spell in the hill saddle, many things had happened.

The Americans, for instance, who should have been somewhere in the region which he was searching, had been quietly pulled out and relocated in the Sedjenane valley, north of the British positions. The French, using mules for transport, were moving in to take the place of the Americans, but their progress was, of necessity, slow.

Rommel had boldly stopped an orthodox frontal attack by the Eighth Army against the strong defensive line at Mareth, between the Matmata Mountains and the Gulf of Gabes.

Even while the trio were searching for friendly lines and friendly faces, Allied troops were relieving their weary comrades in the saddle below the pinnacle. Two days went by, during which they skirted what they took to be a German strong point.

A good three miles south of the main ridge, they slipped over another one which was lower and smoother. It was a little after dawn, and their water bottles were empty. As they straightened up and looked below them all three shot out a hand and pointed to a leaping torrent of fresh water coasting down the hillside from a spring.

'How about that then, Nick?' the Welshman asked.

The food which they had been able to carry with them was finished. In a way, they didn't mind because it had been bulky and heavy, and anyway, their unlimited supply of vitamin tablets kept them going. But vitamins did nothing to offset a raging thirst, and Billy Thomas suffered through being parched more than the other two.

His eyes rounded and glistened as he looked down at it. 'Just like Welsh mountain water,' he enthused.

'I'd like it better with a froth on it,' Red admitted easily.

'All right, you two go down and drink your fill. Then fill all the water bottles. And leave the Bren up here with me.'

Red and Billy, shaggier than ever now, glanced at one another. It bothered them that Nick's intuitiveness prevented him from trotting down the hill to the water with them. Also that he thought they might be jumped while taking a drink. They said nothing about his instructions. Red surrendered the Bren, and that was that. Nick watched them bound down to the lower level with the water bottles.

He wondered what he was bothering about, and whether the protracted spell in the hills had ruined his nervous system. There was a fairly long, almost straight stretch of the stream below him. About two hundred yards up from where the boys were heading, it went out of sight round a slight curve overhung with bushes and grass.

All innocent, it seemed. Nick glanced off to his left, and then to his right. He pushed himself up from the slope and looked lower down than the stream. Nothing. And yet the little intercostal muscles of his rib cage had seized up.

Billy waved two water bottles round his head, and then plunged his round fair-bearded face into the water. Red waited a second or two longer. He leapt the width of the stream and plunged his face in directly opposite. Billy drank the longer of the two by about five seconds. He came up gasping and grinned hugely into the face of Red which was liberally camouflaged with freckles and sandy growth.

'Go on, you ruddy old camel,' the latter remarked. 'You'll be developin' humps soon!'

The Welsh lad never voiced his reply. From the place where the stream went out of sight came a deadly stream of heavy tracer, fired with superb accuracy. Thomas tipped into the water first with his trunk riddled. Red was hit just as badly as he tried to throw himself into the water for protection.

Before Nick could tear his gaze away from the scene of the tragedy he saw the waters briefly turned red with bood. Then he was up and the Bren was being fired from his hip. One solitary German trooper lurched into view and collapsed, but several others were shouting as Bren ammunition ripped amongst the concealing shrubs and scythed a path through them.

Nick cut short his burst and ran for the crest of the ridge. The weight of the Bren soon had him almost gagging for breath, but he would not stop. A counter burst sent him lunging for the soil, but he did not stay inactive. He pulled from his pouch a grenade and removed the pin. Although the distance was greater than he would normally have attempted, an all-possessing anger added power to his arm.

The pineapple was still dropping over the hidden enemy when it exploded. Unknown to the thrower, two men were killed and one wounded as a result of it. Nick jumped the ridge, and a short burst of bullets. He dropped on the other side, took two minutes to recover his breath, and set off towards the east. That way was Kraut way for sure, but at this stage, having lost his pals, he did not care. It was them or him, and he had weapons, food and some energy left.

He kept close to the ridge and edged up to it again some four hundred yards further along. He glanced over and spotted a German helmet about ten yards below. He backed away, found a spot between two boulders some four or five feet below the crest, and there he folded himself.

The face under the helmet was broad. It boasted a thick hooked nose and a non-existent pair of lips. Nick saw it at the angle from which Mussolini always had his photographs taken before he swiftly uncoiled and struck upwards, under the rib cage with his knife.

The dying man came over the crest at though he was making heavy going of the climb. He was assisted down to a firm resting place. His helmet was removed for use as a temporary water bottle, and within five minutes his killer had recrossed the ridge and slaked his thirst.

17

From that time onwards, Nick stopped actively looking for Allies and sought only Axis troops. In his searching he found them. He topped up his energy with the vitamin pills from that canister drop and drank when he could. The very next day, he came upon upwards of a score of German soldiers sleeping in a cave. From the mouth of it he blasted them with the Bren. Many tried to crawl away, or to grab their weapons, but the resting place had no other way out and no boulders behind which a man could hide.

Nick was still firing after the shouts and cries had ceased. The emptying of the magazine finally stopped him. He found then that it was of no further use to him because he was out of ammunition. So he abandoned it, and chose for himself a modern German machine-gun heavier than his Sten, but not yet so heavy as the Bren. He also helped himself to a few items of food and a map which purported to be of the immediate surroundings.

He moved eastward in short marches and climbs. On several occasions, he crossed and recrossed the sinewy backbone of the hills and always he was on the alert to make his presence felt. On one occasion, he blasted a huge rock down onto a beautiful, though narrow hill road and completely blocked it.

Three days later, he placed explosives under a wooden bridge which spanned a gap between sections of mountain road in the adjacent valley. By the time a motorized column column started to pass over it he was out of sighting distance. Alas, for the column. The first vehicle touched off the explosives. It crashed through the bridge and took with it four and twenty untried young warriors newly recruited to a crack division who had not been afforded the chance to win an Iron Cross 2nd Class. Those who followed behind had to wait on a road which offered no shelter for a time which seemed interminable, until the engineers could be driven to the spot.

At the end of that same week, the lonely sergeant wandered down to a track which permitted motorized vehicles. With his German helmet on his head he walked into a small hamlet where six Italian Lancias were drawn up outside what appeared to be a transport cafe. The troops and the drivers were inside, behind windows fogged up by steam. All except one, who looked to be a misfit.

This lone driver smoked a drooping cigarette, with an elbow resting on the radiator of his truck. Nick walked right up to him, pointing to his own unlit cigarette and leaned towards the driver. As soon as his cigarette was lit, he hit the unfortunate man over the back of the head with the butt of his German gun and lifted him back into the cab.

One after another, the engines of the lorries received his attention. By this time, he was out of explosives, but it was easy to render the trucks useless by removing a small vital part from under the bonnet. By the time his cigarette was half smoked, the first of the travellers had wandered as far as the door.

Putting his head down to ward off the rain, he walked out with a swinging stride which soon took him beyond the hamlet into isolation. Needless to say, he soon left the track and hid himself in higher broken ground.

Unknown to Nick, the German fighting calculated to waste time before the international contest was switched to Europe, had almost run its course. At Mareth, in the south, Montgomery had cleverly outwitted Rommel by switching the main thrust of his forces, held at the defensive line, to a big out-flanking movement to westward of the battle and carried out by New Zealanders backed by the greater part of the armour.

The New Zealanders had moved westward of the Matmata Mountains and cut in south of a salt lake and more hills to hit the Afrika Korps at El Hamma, west of Gabes on the coast. Rommel's élite forces had been bested and the withdrawal had not been any too easy. A wonderful air coverage had helped the flank thrust, and hearty co-operation from the Americans further north had kept German support armour out of the contest.

The Allied ring was tightening around the German positions wide of Tunis and Bizerta. The British were almost ready to oust the tenacious Germans from the key hills at the eastern end of their sector, and the Americans were striving to keep track of the advance further north.

Spring was improving the state of the hills. Although he knew nothing of all the cheering news in military circles, Nick found he could sleep better, and here and there he was able to gather some of the first wild fruit of the year, and thus implement his rather colourless iron diet.

At times, his thoughts were none too clear. He brooded over absent friends; comrades in arms who had lost their lives through trusting him and obeying his orders. Sometimes he felt he was the victim of a conspiracy. One which had been started to get him to see things the Army's way, and to take on responsibility when he hadn't wanted any. He saw that dark-haired captain in Algiers, the one who had claimed to have been at college with Harry, as a conspirator; a man who had been instructed to tell Nick certain things to make a reliable Army man of him. He felt that his brother, Harry, was not in Tunisia at all, and that it had only been suggested he was in the area to lure him — Nick — on to brighter and better things. He even admitted to himself that he was not really looking for Harry, that he didn't expect to make contact with him.

But after this personal brain-washing, he felt nonplussed, not knowing what he was about; having no clear purpose in life. And then he would see signs of the enemy and tell himself with great deliberation that he *had* a purpose and that was to overthrow the enemy, German or Italian, in large or small numbers.

Then his energy was restored and his powers of constructive thought returned. The days slipped by and added up to weeks, and still he was one man at large, isolated from his own kind.

★   ★   ★

285

One day, which he took to be in the month of April, he was seated on the side of a hill to westward of the town of Zaghouan. He used his binoculars to make clearer the events which were taking place east of Zaghouan in the comparatively flat land between the mountains and the Gulf of Hammamet. During the whole of the previous day, tanks, lorries and scout cars, in fact, vehicles of every description, had been moving steadily towards the north. Even with glasses it was not absolutely clear to which side they belonged. The Germans had contested North Africa with the British for so long that both armies used trucks captured from the other side. But Nick had developed a special kind of patience. He stayed on his high hill and watched.

Late in the afternoon of the previous day, he had seen an unmistakable German staff car pull in at a small hamlet tucked in at the foot of the Zaghouan hills. Now, he perceived that it was still there. Moreover, there were positive signs that it might be coming up the winding road which lead near to where the lone

Englishman was sitting.

He watched a feldwebel wave on several vehicles loaded with other Germans, denying them the right to stop in that place. The officer whose car it was, came out from a café where he had spent the night, and began to pace up and down with his hands behind his back. He was a tall plump man in a smart greatcoat and a peaked cap which stood high on his forehead. Presently, this officer grew impatient.

The feldwebel ran to get in the car and sit beside the driver. The officer clambered into the back, and two younger officers joined him. The car's exhaust gave out a cloud of smoke. It surged forward and came straight up the hill road. Every few minutes, Nick caught glimpses of the car and its occupants. He began to think that he was fated to make contact with them.

The road faded out, ran to nothing, within a furlong of Nick's position. Perceiving that the staff car would be forced to stop at the top, he worked his way through shrubs and grass until he was about fifty yards below the road end. Presently the car arrived, and the retinue leapt out and opened the door for the senior officer, who was a colonel. He nodded to them, ignoring their saluting, and walked off on his own, polishing a pair of rimless spectacles which he took from his pocket. He stepped off the lower side of the road, walked a few yards down the slope and stood at ease, facing the east with the spectacles on his nose.

Nick watched him, and wondered about this strange meeting. A mere few days back, the meeting might have been altogether different. The men who had come up in that car might have been annihilated by his fine automatic weapon before they left their seats.

Now, the driver, the N.C.O. and the two young officers had wandered away from the vehicle to smoke and talk. Obviously, a change had taken place in the basic thinking of the young man who might have confounded them. He wondered how he should behave, what his conduct should be towards this senior officer who had come up a remote road for the sake of solitude, or for something more sinister.

He decided that he would kidnap the colonel. Take him below at the point of a weapon manufactured in his own country. An officer of this one's rank would be a sort of insurance for when Nick might run into alert forces of the enemy.

His brain started to make plans. He made a definite click with his weapon.

'Kolonel, if you value your life you will not make a sound. Nor will you attempt to contact your subordinates! Do you understand? I have a gun trained on you!'

'*Jawohl, Herr Englander*. What do you want of me?'

Nick blinked. He realized after receiving this reply in impeccable English that he had expected the colonel to understand him. The fellow not only understood him, but spoke better English than he did himself.

'You are my prisoner. I require you to step down towards me, and to continue slowly down the hillside. And please don't make any tricky moves because my nerves are not quite as good as they were at the beginning of the campaign. Come now.'

The colonel had a formidable jaw, a strong nose and brows like a British pilot's wings insignia. The grey eyes behind the lenses seemed hurt, rather than afraid. 'Tell me, Sergeant, do you think this is necessary at this stage of the campaign?'

'Of course it's necessary. Now, get moving!'

The prisoner complied, walking steadily down the slope and using his wits to keep from stumbling. Nick shared his attention between his prisoner and the end of the road where the vehicle was still in sight. When they had gone about one hundred yards, a useful crop of rocks, almost chest high, partially concealed them. Just as the edginess started to ease in Nick's troubled mind, there was a shout from above and two Schmeissers opened up rather wildly in the direction of the absconding pair.

A fusillade of bullets came near, and yet none of them appeared to find a human mark. The colonel appeared to turn his ankle. He staggered for a second and then recovered. So did Nick. The latter sprang towards his prisoner and poked the stolen Schmeisser into his side.

The firing above stopped. Nick waved a hand at the two junior officers with the weapons, and the others who crouched near them.

'Go away! If you fire again, I shall kill your Kolonel!'

For several seconds, the colonel's men stayed quite still, apparently still shocked by the sudden turn of events. Without warning, the prisoner shouted something to them, and this time they obeyed instantly. They backed off and remained hidden from view. Nick snapped at his prisoner.

'I meant what I said. If they come after us, you'll be dead when they catch up.'

The colonel appeared to have paled. 'Have no fears, Sergeant. I merely repeated your instructions. They won't come after us.'

Nick prodded his victim down the slope for several hundred feet before he felt wholly assured. Then, as his mental attitude changed, he began to take stock of the colonel. He removed the weapon from his side.

'I — er, I'm Sergeant Nick Burrows of

the Red Devils, Kolonel. Cut off from our boys in the British salient.'

'How do you do? I'm Kolonel Fritz Johann Adler, at your service.'

He was about to say more, but the griping pain in his right shoulder began to take its toll of him. When his men opened up, he had been struck by a ricochet. He admitted as much, and Nick felt suddenly tired and baffled.

'I captured you as a kind of insurance,' he explained. 'That wound of yours, unfortunately, makes a hell of a difference.'

Nick produced his action wound dressing. He made a wad of some of the bandaging and helped to pad the colonel's shoulder. A half hour later, he found a shallow cave and assisted the wounded man into it. Between them they stripped off the greatcoat and the tunic and laid the shoulder bare.

Nick frowned at the seeping wound. 'You should have told me about it earlier,' he grumbled. 'The bullet will have to be removed.'

In his late fifties, Kolonel Adler had

achieved a certain serenity which the war had been unable to alter. He awaited Nick's pronouncements and seemed to approve when he built a fire and set about making a dry comfortable place where a man could lie flat. Nick boiled water and gave his slim-bladed knife a thorough cleansing. He hesitated before starting the painful business of probing, a job at which he had no previous experience.

Adler nodded and smiled, and after ten minutes of patient effort, Nick removed the flattened bullet and tossed it aside. He strapped up the shoulder, after bandaging it with great care. The patient's eyebrows went up when he was given a German-issue cigarette. He lay back on the couch of dry grass and heather and blew smoke with great satisfaction.

'I'll have to get you to a proper doctor without delay, Herr Kolonel. You've lost a lot of blood and there's still a seepage coming from your shoulder.'

Adler gestured with the cigarette. 'I shall survive, Sergeant. Don't foul up your plans on my account.'

Something in this calmness rattled

Nick. 'You talk as if I wanted to stay in these hills! Believe me, I've had enough. The thing is I've no clear picture of the war situation further east.'

Adler looked surprised. '*Herr Gott!* But it's almost finished, Sergeant. Tunis and Bizerta fell several days ago. Rommel is out of the country, and General Von Arnim, the C.-in-C. has probably surrendered by now. I came away out of it to try and get a little peace before giving myself up.'

Suspicion glinted in Nick's eyes. 'You could be telling me an awful lie, Kolonel. If what you say is true, why did your men back there bother to shoot?'

'They were concerned for my safety. Perhaps more so than I am. I sent them away because there is no further need for them to risk their lives. A good officer is always conscious of the risks his men take. It is good to be able to tell them to desist, now and again.'

These words made sense to Nick, albeit bitter sense. He thought of the friends who had died obeying his instructions. Particularly, he was remembering Jock,

Ginger and Pongo. He shrugged as though to push away bad memories.

He said: 'Get some sleep, Kolonel. We'll look for transport tomorrow.'

But neither of them felt like sleeping, and without knowing quite how or why, Nick launched into a narrative of his adventures since the war in Tunisia began. He fell asleep with his head on his chest, eventually, and Adler dozed some time later.

* * *

Between ten and eleven the following morning, the alert British sergeant with his prisoner waved down a jeep which was speeding along the Pont du Fahs-Zaghouan road. In charge of it was a corporal of the Recce Corps. He seemed disinclined to give a lift to the sergeant, and unimpressed by the rank of his prisoner. He was seriously thinking of driving on and leaving them where they were.

Nick started to bring up his Schmeisser, and Kolonel Adler looked as if he might protest, but it was the driver who actually broke the deadlock. He whispered something to the N.C.O., who asked: 'What did you say your name was, Sergeant?'

'Nick Burrows, but what that's got to do with the situation I can't imagine!'

''Ave you got a brother in our outfit. A Captain?'

Nick nodded. He was still prepared for trouble, but the corporal's craggy face suddenly broke out into a grin. He signalled for them to get in the back. Nick, as baffled as his prisoner, got in and kept a watchful eye on the N.C.O. and the driver as they sped up the road and eventually turned into a lesser one.

The driver stopped the jeep outside an adobe-style inn. His corporal had a quiet word with a man on guard outside. Adler followed Nick indoors. The sergeant knocked on a door in the passage, was called in, and saluted a bulky, round-faced moustached officer who was forty-eight hours away from a shave and looking a trifle harassed.

The captain lurched to his feet,

embarrassed by the smart salute. He rasped a thumb nail round his fair stubble and returned the compliment.

'Sergeant Burrows of the Parachute Regiment, sir. And Kolonel Adler, a prisoner needing medical aid.'

Harry Burrows was speechless for almost half a minute. Suddenly the brothers came together and embraced. Adler stepped to one side and waited. He was later removed into a small private room which held an iron bedstead and a mattress. Harry promised to bring in the first medical doctor passing through, and made him comfortable.

The older brother slumped back into his desk chair, and kicked an easier one towards Nick, who sat down in it and felt more relaxed than he had done for a very long time. He took a proffered glass of cognac and they drank to each other's health, and then to peace in North Africa.

Motor cyclists kept bringing in messages, and other items of information came over the radio. Nick listened, and quite soon it became clear to him that everything Adler had told him was correct. The most staggering piece of information to come over the radio had to do with tens of thousands of Germans milling around in the Bir Peninsular looking for someone to whom they could surrender.

The Royal Navy prevented their getting away by sea, and the R.A.F. controlled the skies. It was almost like the conclusion of a nightmare which had turned pleasant. Almost too convenient.

Harry said: 'It's good to see you, lad, and congratulations on getting a set of stripes.'

'Thanks, Harry, it's good to see you, too. And congratulations on becoming a father.' He hesitated, and then went on. 'There was a time when I thought meeting up with you would be something extra special. Now, I'm afraid it's fallen rather flat.'

'Did you feel at one time that you *had* to find me?' Harry asked shrewdly.

Nick nodded and sipped more of his cognac.

Harry went on: 'I don't think you were ever really looking for me. You were looking for yourself. Moreover, I think you've caught up with yourself. You've changed. You look more mature, and it isn't just the beard, either. You've grown up.'

Nick savoured these words of wisdom. Within minutes he had slipped off into a deep doze. Heavy boots going out awoke him. Harry was pacing the floor, smoking a cigarette and looking amused. He came to Nick's side as the latter yawned and rubbed his eyes.

'That was the doctor just leaving. That Kraut you picked up is quite a fellow. He's an ex-archaeologist. Wants to recommend you to the appropriate authorities for a commission. I told him it was a bit unusual for a prisoner to make recommendations, and pointed out that it would be embarrassing seeing that we were brothers.

'He wouldn't be put off, though, and he's writing his recommendations out on paper with his left hand. I suppose I could pass it on. After all, he's quite genuine.'

Nick's restless eyes wandered all over

the room. 'You're not just saying that, Harry? I mean, do you really think I could hold down a commission? Wear pips and all?'

'It's sometimes harder to hold down three stripes than it is to wear pips, Nick. Sure you could do it. Anyway, Europe will tell.'

Nick started. 'Eh? What was that?'

'Europe. The next theatre of war.'

Nick said: 'Oh.' He nodded several times. He went off to sleep again.

We do hope that you have enjoyed reading this large print book.

Did you know that all of our titles are available for purchase?

We publish a wide range of high quality large print books including:

Romances, Mysteries, Classics
General Fiction
Non Fiction and Westerns

Special interest titles available in large print are:

The Little Oxford Dictionary
Music Book, Song Book
Hymn Book, Service Book

Also available from us courtesy of Oxford University Press:

Young Readers' Dictionary
(large print edition)
Young Readers' Thesaurus
(large print edition)

For further information or a free brochure, please contact us at:
Ulverscroft Large Print Books Ltd.,
The Green, Bradgate Road, Anstey,
Leicester, LE7 7FU, England.
Tel: (00 44) **0116 236 4325**
Fax: (00 44) **0116 234 0205**

RICOCHET

J. F. Straker

John Everard is a cold, ruthless businessman. When he returns home from a business trip he discovers that his Spanish wife Juanita and baby son Tommy have disappeared, his house has been burgled, and his firm's payroll stolen. Moreover, it was his wife who was seen driving the thieves away in Everard's own Jaguar. Has Juanita been kidnapped — or is she implicated in the robbery? And where is Tommy? Now, with little police co-operation, Everard begins his own investigation . . .

FOOL'S PARADISE

John Russell Fearn

In a fit of pique, Milly Morton — confidential 'secretary' to industrialist Mortimer Bland — deliberately smashed the astronomical plates of Bland's Chief Scientist, Anton Drew. Furthermore, she'd destroyed data which would warn the world of a forthcoming cosmic disaster. The unprecedented violent storms, signs of approaching doom, went unrecognized. Eventually Drew, aided by his friends Ken and Thayleen West, convinced the Prime Minister of the danger — but would it be too late to save the world?

DEATH COMES CALLING

John Glasby

In Los Angeles, the wealthy Marcia Edwards asks investigator Johnny Merak to find her missing grandson. Merak suspects it's a mob kidnapping. There's someone else who wants to hire him: the model Angela Cliveden, who has been receiving life-threatening phone calls. Merak discovers that she is the girlfriend of Tony Minello of the local Mafia. But when she is found murdered in her apartment, Merak is trapped in a potential Mob War and matching his wits with a cunning serial killer.

DEVIL'S PEAK

Brian Ball

Stranded in a High Peak transport café during a freak snowstorm, Jerry Howard finds himself in a vortex of Satanism. Brenda was a motorway girl with a strange scar on her back. The Mark of the Beast. She knew the history of the Brindley legend. And she alone knew the rites. She had been on Devil's Peak before. Now it was Walpurgisnacht and the horned goat was expected. Events moved to a horrendous climax . . .

DEATH ON DORADO

John Light

When wealthy businessman Edlin Borrowitch is murdered, Tec Sarn Denson is called in to defend the woman accused of the killing, Ros Kernwell. The case is a puzzling one and Denson finds her innocence difficult to prove. However, the one thing he doesn't lack is a list of suspects — but when everyone has a motive for murder, how can he choose? And how can he stay alive when the murderer is out to get him too?